T5-CCU-389

The SIMIAN BRIDGE

A Novel

by Ray DiZazzo

CAMBRIDGE HOUSE PRESS
NEW YORK

Published by
Cambridge House Press
New York, NY 10001
www.camhousepress.com

Cover design by Chris Stribley.
Book design by Rachel Trusheim.

Library of Congress Cataloging-in-Publication Data

DiZazzo, Raymond.
The Simian bridge : a novel / by Ray DiZazzo.
p. cm.
ISBN 978-0-9814536-7-5
I. Title.

PS3604.I98S56 2009
813'.6--dc22

2008053398

10 9 8 7 6 5 4 3 2 1

Printed in the United States of America.

To those who search.

"A man who has no words will tell the story."

—Kenya Scrolls

BIRTH

Throughout much of the year, the ground in Ethiopia is tan and hard from long days of baking under the equatorial sun. Crops resist growth in such earth, and the wind carries in curtains of dust, leaving the bushes brittle and leafless. Many people go hungry in these times, and the old and young die like the withered grasses.

It was onto Ethiopia's hard, sweltering floor, in the shade of a small grove of acacia trees that Cheliese Olafa came into the world. Her glistening, dark brown, seven-pound body should have slid from her mother's womb in the privacy of the birthing house, just as her five siblings had. That had been her family's intent, but, as was often the case in this part of the world, nature had intervened.

In spite of two severe drought years, several disease outbreaks, and a slight deformity that made her right foot stiff and caused her to limp, Cheliese grew healthy and strong. By the time her fifth birthday passed, she had become an accomplished weaver and helper who cleaned well and carried water and made things from the bush into things for the living. In her seventh year, her father fell under a bull and died from a broken neck. This loss did not make Cheliese particularly sad because she had never been close to, or comfortable with, her father. Most times she was afraid in his presence and the only physical contact she'd had with him was disciplinary and violent.

Cheliese loved her mother deeply, however, and when the old woman passed away from malaria just after Cheliese's tenth birthday, the girl wailed with heartbreak and went by herself into the bush for two days.

It was during this time that the dreams began.

ONE

Mitchell Solomon stepped from the elevator into a small marble atrium on the seventeenth floor of the Ames-Corialis building, and moving through frosted glass doors etched with a sweeping, cityscape logo, paused momentarily to ponder the Waltrick Media Management company name beneath it. It was a name, he recalled, that had been a part of his career dream five years earlier when he'd completed his degree at Harvard Law. Whether it was representing executives at one of the major studios, hammering out multimillion dollar mergers and partnerships, or simply grinding the competition into bankruptcy, Waltrick was the undisputed eight-hundred-pound gorilla of media law.

Solomon had come to the firm as hungry and capable as any of the young junior attorneys. He'd jumped right in and left his share of blood in the water almost immediately, and at Waltrick that was recognized with money and access to power. He'd gotten introductions to key players very quickly, including founder Sam Waltrick, pulled off some impressive feats before the Bench, and eventually moved to the Porsche and Lamborghini end of southern California's plush Hidden Valley.

When things had changed for Solomon he wasn't sure. Nor did he completely understand why. He only knew that at some fairly recent point in his tenure at Waltrick something had happened that he couldn't quite put his finger on—something odd that had made him lose the stomach for it.

Approaching Sam Waltrick's secretary, Solomon took in the huge teak desk, the fresh flowers, the heavy smell of leather and expensive perfume.

"Hello, Mr. Solomon," the secretary said, with a slight sympathetic pout of her bright red lips. "He's on a conference call. He'll be right with you."

"Thank you, Leslie," Solomon responded with a confident nod that both he and she knew was a façade. He then took a seat on the leather couch, drew a long deep breath, and picked up a copy of the *Wall Street Journal* from the leaded glass table before him.

"Look, Sam," the voice on the other end of the line said, "I'll be straight. We're just not going to let you do it. We're playing hardball on this one."

Sam Waltrick chuckled, shook his head and stepped away from his panoramic, office window view of the Los Angeles metro area. He moved to his desk, took a seat across from his vice president of mergers and winked at the executive. The vice president smiled.

"Well, since we're being straight," Sam said, "let me get straight to the point, John. Never in your existence have you guys been capable of stopping me from doing anything. Nor will you ever be. You have a good few years out there in 'Podunk City' and suddenly, you think you're the top dogs."

"Not a few good years, Sam, a good decade. And don't give me that 'Sam Waltrick king of the hill' bullshit. This time we got there first, and pal, you're locked out. You're simply not going to do it, my friend. Sorry."

"I've got news for you," Sam said. "It's done. Check with your people in Tokyo. Oh, and by the way, why don't you give that idiotic hardball speech to Markel and Dawson? They both jumped ship overnight. They're with us now."

The line went silent.

Again Sam chuckled. "Keep up the good work, John," he said. "You'll get there, 'pal.'" He then pushed the speakerphone button, disconnecting the call, and said to his vice president, "Get the hell over there and finish up, Andy. That asshole pisses me off."

TWO

Out in the foyer, Mitchell Solomon checked his watch: 6:55 a.m. The massive mahogany doors at the far end of the room swung open. Sam and the vice president stepped out shaking hands. "That's fine," Sam was saying, "and do me a favor. Pick up a case of big league hardballs. We'll sign a bunch and send 'em to Wilson and his senior team." The two shared a laugh and the vice president stepped away.

Sam turned his long, pointed face and looked Solomon's way. The CEO's tall, lean frame struck an immaculate business image in black wool slacks and a navy blue crewneck. His ultra-short gray hair combed forward flat, added to the charismatic air of a Hollywood mogul. "Mitch," he said in a light, friendly tone, "come on in."

Solomon got to his feet. "Hi, Sam," he said, struggling to keep his voice from quavering. As he entered the office Sam patted him on the back. The friendly tone was replaced by a serious business demeanor as he said, "I'm glad you could meet with us. Bill's here, too. Coffee?"

"No, thanks," Solomon responded as he looked to his right and saw the stout, muscular figure of his immediate boss. He was seated across the room on a white couch behind a glass coffee table. His jacket was off, but his tie was cinched up tight and, as usual, his white shirt was heavily starched. In front of him was a neatly placed arrangement—a notepad and a folder spread open beside a china cup and saucer. He got to his feet, extending a thick, stubby hand as Solomon approached.

"Have a seat, Mitch," he said.

Solomon did so.

Sam took a seat in the chair across from the couch.

As Solomon had expected, it didn't take Sam long. He thought for a second and then began, "I brought you in this morning, Mitchell, to discuss your future. Bill and I—"

Suddenly he was cut off by an intercom tone.

For an instant he appeared startled, almost as if insulted by some vulgar remark. His eyebrows scrunched, and he began to cock his head as if to say, "What in God's name has gotten into Leslie, cutting me off like this?" But in the next split second he caught himself. His expression eased back into that of the unflappable, tough-as-nails CEO.

He'd realized something, Solomon thought. Of course! The water cooler rumors! A call had probably come from the one and only person Sam Waltrick supposedly allowed to interrupt him in important meetings—his wife!

Sam hit the button on the telephone beside him. "Yes, Leslie," he said.

"I'm sorry to disturb you, Mr. Waltrick. Line six."

Sam hesitated for a moment.

Leslie continued, "The caller is...aware of your busy schedule, sir."

The secretary had hesitated as she spoke. Solomon wondered if her words were a coded message of some sort. A moment later, he knew he was right.

Sam looked down, quickly gathered his thoughts, and then looked back up into Solomon's eyes. "I'd wanted to spend more time with you, Mitch," he said, "but we'll have to make this quick. Both Bill and I have been concerned about your performance. I'm sure you know that. I understand he's had several discussions with you. We've decided it's time to part ways. Bill had wanted to do this himself, but I asked that we meet with you together. You've done some very good things for this company and I wanted to say I appreciate that. I'd like your letter of resignation on my desk today, and you can be sure we'll send you off comfortably."

Solomon considered saying something in his defense, but he knew it would be futile. He also knew Sam was right. So, he simply said, "Okay."

Sam got to his feet. Solomon and his boss did likewise. Sam reached across the desk and shook hands with Solomon. "You're a good man, Mitch," he said. "And I don't mean that just in a work sense. You're a good man at heart. Maybe that's the problem."

Solomon smiled weakly. Just as he was turning to leave, Sam had an afterthought. He turned back. Something had changed in the CEO's expression. Odd, Solomon thought. He wasn't sure what had just happened. "I have a feeling this law business isn't your calling," Sam said, breaking Solomon's train of thought. "I think you'll make your mark, but in some other way."

"Thank you," Solomon said, wincing from the suggestion that he should get out of the business entirely. He then turned and walked out. His boss quickly gathered up his things and followed.

The moment the door closed, the air of executive command drained from Sam Waltrick's face and posture. He sat down, lowered his head into his hands, and let out a deep breath. For a long moment, he sat quietly rubbing his temples, eyes closed, breathing slowly. Then he reached for line six, picked it up and, in a flat, weary tone, said, "Hi."

Alice Waltrick knew that although her husband could strike fear in the hearts of senior executives, the one thing he could not do was leave her waiting. No matter how important the business, she knew that if she called and told Leslie that she hated to bother him because she knew how busy his schedule was, he would answer in a moment.

Alice was also aware of how special this privilege was. She had only used it twice that she could remember. The first occasion had been to let Sam know his father had just suffered a heart attack. The second was to inform him that their daughter, Jennifer, had been accepted to Northwestern University.

This time, when Sam picked up the phone, in a quavering voice she said, "Sam, Christopher just called. He's in Africa! We have to go to him right away!"

THREE

Earlier that morning, Alice had sat down to crochet in a favorite wicker chair facing the large, center bay window in her grand room. Glancing up occasionally through the five-by-eight-foot pane of glass, she'd watched the black, pre-dawn sky pale to deep gray above an oak and eucalyptus tree line.

A storm was approaching.

Despite the dark, ominous cover of first light, her thoughts had been peaceful. Her usual feelings of anxiety had been absent, and she'd noticed that the tremors in her hands were nearly imperceptible.

With both hands working so well, she had decided to put the finishing touches on the baby sweater she had started crocheting three weeks earlier for a friend's daughter. She'd just begun threading a tiny pink ribbon through the collar of the sweater, when the phone on the table beside her rang. She placed the sweater on her lap and brushed over it with her palm, luxuriating in its cool softness. She picked up the receiver and said, "Hello?"

"Hi, Mom."

She clutched the sweater. "Christopher! My God, how are you, honey?"

"I'm fine. How are you?"

"I'm fine, sweetheart! How long has it been? Six months?"

"Yeah. I guess, about that."

"Where are you? What are you doing?"

He paused momentarily. "I'm in Africa."

"Africa! What on earth are you doing there?"

He paused again. "I found this amazing place, Mom. Actually, some friends took me there."

"Place." That was a key word, Alice knew. And so was "friends." Christopher had a way of finding odd places and making odd friends. As she thought back, she felt the familiar knots of discomfort begin to tighten in her stomach.

Two years ago it had been a group of artists in New York. Seven of them living in a basement. They sold their work on street corners, gave every cent to Green Peace, panhandled for food and shared possessions—including sexual partners. Six months later, it was Mexico. He had found a village on the outskirts of the popular resort of Ixtapa, which was filled year round with tourists from all corners of the globe. His cause in that instance had been what he called the "resort slave labor" many of the local people had been forced to accept as a way of life. Then came the weekend in jail for use of LSD, the activist marches, and political demonstrations—the never-ending quest to rebel from virtually everything society accepted as the norm.

"What kind of place?" Alice asked. "And who are these people?"

"I'd rather not tell you over the phone, Mom. I'd rather show you."

Alice was stunned. An invitation?

"You...and especially Dad. Maybe even Jenn and Jesse."

Especially Dad? Something was definitely up. She wasn't sure what, but to Christopher it was something big. "You mean you'd like us to *visit?*"

"Right."

"But, Christopher, you know your dad is—"

"I know, he's always busy. But this is important."

She sensed something deeper in his words. "Important?"

"Yes, I, look, I can't tell you all about it on the phone. But there's a place, Mom, a bridge. A very special and incredible bridge that leads to... Look, I know Dad and I haven't been... I know I've caused you both some problems. But I want you to come here and experience this."

"But, honey, your dad and I—"

"I know about his schedule, Mom."

"Maybe sometime soon. I'm not sure, honey."

"I may not be seeing you two, the family...again."

Alice waited for the end of the sentence, "seeing you two, the family, again *until...*" When that word didn't come, for a moment she thought he'd just forgotten to say it. She even started to finish the sentence for him, uttering, "unt—"

Then something else occurred to her—something horrifying: "seeing you again *ever*"? Is that what he meant? "What?" she said, her voice beginning to quaver.

"Mom, I'm going someplace. Someplace I may not be able to come back from. I love you both very much, and I'd like to give you…a gift before I leave."

Alice felt the blood drain from her face.

FOUR

At 6:50 a.m., Carol Drey was just entering the Constellation Wing of the Waltrick home. She noticed Alice approaching from down the long hall that led to the rest of the house. Carol veered to her right, passed Maria Escobar, her assistant, and met Alice.

"Hi, Carol," Alice said.

And just as when Alice had spoken to Christopher and sensed something was wrong, Carol, too, immediately heard something ominous in her friend's voice. "Everything okay?" she asked.

"Actually, no. Not really. I just got a call from Christopher."

"What now?"

"He's in some sort of trouble in Africa, of all places."

"Africa! My God!"

Quietly, Alice said, "Sam and I are going to have to go for a few days."

It was then that Carol sensed real trouble. "It's nothing *too* serious, is it?"

"He seemed, I don't know, not himself, I guess. How's Jesse?"

"He's fine. He's probably just waking up."

"We'll be leaving tomorrow," Alice said, "and I'm afraid he might sense something if I see him right now."

"You go take care of whatever you need to," Carol said. "And tell that hard-headed world traveler of yours I'm going to kick his butt when I see him!"

The attempt at humor failed. "I will," Alice said with a worried smile.

"And don't worry about your number two son. Jesse will be fine. As long as I'm with him, he gets nothing but love."

Alice smiled weakly. "Well," she said, "I have to call Sam now. He's in the middle of meetings, and I'm about to make his morning very unpleasant."

When Alice left, Carol crossed the pale blue carpet through an octagonal atrium that was the center of the Constellation Wing. She turned right. Entering Jesse's room, she stepped into a large area of leafy foliage, under an immense Plexiglas ceiling. Wooden panels had accordioned back on both sides, leaving the entire ceiling open to the gray morning sky. Despite the many trees and palms, one side of the room resembled a large classroom with only two desks. On the walls were colorful animal shapes and drawings of clouds and rainbows. A chalkboard and alphabet poster covered part of one wall and whimsical, cartoon characters gave a festive, storybook feel to the entire space.

She found the boy lying awake in bed. In his hands

were two crocheted, stuffed animals his mother had recently made for him—a rabbit and a duck. Jesse had been eyeing both fondly, and whispering quiet sounds to himself. The moment he saw Carol enter the room he stopped talking, put the stuffed animals aside and smiled.

Carol smiled also, saying, "Hi there, kiddo!"

Jesse chuckled and drooled, arms outstretched. Carol knelt and shared a hug, being careful to position herself so his strength wouldn't hurt her neck. "You're my favorite little puppy, kiddo. You know that?"

And, indeed, Carol thought, Jesse was like a large, ungainly puppy. He snuggled his angular body up to her, trying to wedge his head under her chin and almost whining with delight at her presence. Carol looked down. The nineteen-year-old squirmed and the smile on his face had gone. Carol knew what this meant. He had become so excited he'd wet his diaper again.

At first, Cheliese could only wonder what the dreams meant and why they had come to her. They had no women, hunters, farmers, or animals in them. Nor did they depict events or places she could describe. They were made of nothing more than a kind of motion that seemed to speak a strange language. The motion was like a great ebbing and flowing that passed the pieces of a puzzle above and around her. And though she could not clearly see these pieces, she knew they were not like wooden,

cloth, or stone puzzle pieces. They did not fit together the way other pieces fit, but they did somehow belong in a kind of order or harmony—a balance. The language in the dreams contained no words like those that came from the mouths of men and women. It contained no breath or familiar sounds. Rather, it was a language that was somehow a part of the motion she sensed. It seemed to pass around and through her mind in familiar rhythms. As the puzzle pieces sped up or slowed down with the ebb and flow of the rhythms, their movement spoke to her in different ways.

At first, Cheliese thought these dreams were a kind of delirium that had nested in her heart because of the grief she felt for her mother. But as time passed and her heart ached less and less, the dreams did not diminish—especially, she realized, when she slept alone under the night sky.

Over the next two years, she lost two brothers to disease, and at the age of fourteen she was married. Serving her husband well, and working very hard for her family, she bore eight children. Two died at birth and two more were lost before the age of five. One fell into a ravine, which released something terrible inside his body. He shook and swelled up, turning the color of the ground as Cheliese and her husband tried to help him. Another son was bitten by the black-mouthed snake. This boy, too, convulsed and wailed for hours, passing slowly in Cheliese's arms.

Sadness and happiness came many times over the years, and this made her a wise and strong woman. Because of her wisdom, she never told her husband or friends about her dreams. She knew she might be branded as a witch or a possessed spirit, and perhaps banned from the village and sent to live with the unholy. But she slept under the stars on many nights and the dreams continued. And as many years passed, she began to understand the language they spoke to her. Very slowly, she abandoned her struggle to find words in the dreams. Instead, she learned to simply let the motion flow through her mind like a deep, magical river. She discovered that as the currents swirled and circled through her thoughts they told her things which she could not speak about, because there were no words that could explain these ideas. Perhaps, she thought, my mother is speaking this language in the spirit world and I am to learn it. Perhaps someday we will see each other again and talk in her language about all the years and the pain and happiness. I must learn this language well.

Twelve years later, her husband died. By this time her children were grown. Three had married and begun their own families. Another had gone for wood one day and never returned. Cheliese had aged in good health and now, with less responsibility, she began to sleep out every night and walk into the bush for days at a time. The other men and women of the village felt that she was becoming confused in the head because of her years, but she knew the opposite was true. The deeper she went into the bush and the more nights she slept alone under the stars, the stronger the dreams became and the more she understood them. Eventually, she realized that they were not simply speaking to her. They were telling her the beginning of a story…a very important story that she must be sure was eventually told.

FIVE

As Mitchell Solomon sat in his office composing his letter of resignation, eighteen floors below Sam Waltrick stepped out of the garage level elevator and entered a waiting limousine. Moments later the limo pulled out onto Hill Street. As Sam's longtime driver edged into traffic moving toward the Hollywood freeway, Sam picked up the morning edition of *USA Today* and read the headline, "Muslims Demonstrate, President Defiant." He shook his head, whispered, "Christ, here we go again," and tossed the paper aside. As traffic picked up, he sat quietly, watching the Los Angeles skyline pass by against a backdrop of dark clouds.

The driver noticed Sam's uneasiness. "How are things, Sam?" he asked, glancing in the rear view mirror.

"Fine," Sam responded.

"You finally lose one?"

"We don't lose, Mark. You know that. In fact, we just wrapped up a deal in Japan that will be very lucrative."

"Excellent."

Sam became quiet again. When the driver got no more response, he decided to drop the conversation. A few minutes later Sam broke the silence. "It's that damned kid again."

"Chris?"

"Who else?"

The driver chuckled and shook his head, his plump, freckled face bulging out over his tie and white collar. "Kids!" he exclaimed in a raspy, southern drawl. "They're a pain in the ass, Sam. I don't care what anyone says."

Suddenly Sam's demeanor changed. Like a teacher about to challenge one of his brighter students, he said, "I've got a question for you, Mark."

"Shoot."

"Tell me what's meaningful or constructive about making some of the most selfish, inconsiderate bastards on earth filthy rich, and sending the fools too stupid to figure out how to play the game into bankruptcy?"

This caught the driver off guard. Fumbling for a response, he tried humor. "Personally, I'd consider being filthy rich very meaningful. Trouble is I've never had much luck at it."

Sam didn't answer. Outside, terraced clusters of hillside homes passed by in the gloom. The familiar Hollywood sign became visible in the distance. Intermittent drops of rain had begun leaving streaks on the limo's tinted windows. Finally, Sam continued. "Yesterday I found out a guy we won against two months ago committed suicide."

"Oh, Christ…"

"I went to school with him."

The driver fell silent.

The rain was increasing. Outside, the Universal Studios complex was coming into view. Sam imagined the beaten, hopeless executive placing the barrel of his handgun in his mouth. He wondered how the metal felt against the man's teeth. If his lips had closed around the cold steel. He saw the man's finger on the trigger, curling, pulling...

Turning away from the window, he forced the image from his mind. "I got some *good* news last week. Jennifer was just promoted."

"Good for her!" the driver said, happy to change the subject. "She's a sweetheart."

"Yeah, she'll do well."

"And excuse me for saying so, but as far as I'm concerned you did the right thing when you gave Chris the boot. Kids like him need that kind of push."

Sam remembered it vividly. Just after Chris' twenty-second birthday, he'd had enough. During an argument in which the boy was accusing him of being self-serving and egotistical, he'd called his son an ignorant, ungrateful little son-of-a-bitch and followed with an ultimatum. He remembered the words as if he'd said them yesterday: "If life's become such a terrible experience here at home, you ungrateful little son-of-a-bitch, why the hell are you still here accepting my food, shelter, and money?"

Alice had burst into tears.

Christopher simply turned and quietly left the room.

For the next few days the two didn't speak and a week

later, despite Alice's pleading, Christopher was gone. He'd never come back. That had been three years earlier.

From that point on, the list of idiotic misadventures had begun. He kept in touch through Alice. He called just enough to let them know that he was still alive, and, Sam suspected, in order to secretly borrow money on occasion from Alice. Though Sam was fairly sure this went on, he never mentioned it. He didn't want to put his wife in a situation of having to lie to him or turn down her son. And secretly, it had become a little bit of penance for Sam who had felt, but never let on, that perhaps he should not have allowed himself to lose control that night, no matter how disrespectful his son had been.

"So what's the drill this time?" the driver asked.

"Africa."

"You're kidding!"

"I wish I were."

"What the hell's he doing over there?"

"No idea. Alice said he was involved in something weird and we had to go right away. And get this; she said he specifically asked for me."

The driver smiled, watching Sam in the rear view mirror. "I'll bet the good woman is packing as we speak."

"She'd better not be," Sam said, as the limo made its way off the Hollywood Freeway onto the Ventura Freeway heading west.

SIX

Two calls left, Alice thought as she hung up from Sam. She dialed the first one from where she was sitting.

A machine answered: "Hello, you've reached the office of Dr. Jane Dawson. Our hours are from 9:00 a.m. to 5:00 p.m., Mondays through Fridays. If you'd like to leave a message, please do so after the beep. If this is a crisis, or you need immediate attention, please dial two-two-seven. Thank you."

Alice took a deep breath and made a conscious effort to keep her voice steady and relaxed. "Hi Sealy, this is Alice Waltrick. I'm afraid I'm going to have to cancel this week. Tell Jane I'm fine, I just have to make a quick trip out of town and I'll be back on schedule next week. Thanks."

She then walked into the kitchen, placed her crochet needle and sweater on the breakfast counter, and picked up the shiny, new business card beside the kitchen telephone. It read in part: Jennifer Waltrick, Marketing and Public Relations Manager, Granite-Collen Communications, Inc.

Alice looked at the card, hesitating. Finally, she reached for the phone and dialed.

"Look," Jennifer was saying to one of the company's PR reps, "I don't care what the positioning was. And, Shawn, I don't give a damn about Janice's take on it either. If there's any chance Dora Neil will plug this book on national TV, it's worth giving it a shot. Now send it."

"And what if she says no?"

"Then what have we lost?"

"Maybe our reputation?"

"How? Who finds out? You think Neil is going to strut down Market Street saying, 'Hey guys, Granite-Collen sent me a new novel and it's so bad I won't even read it!'"

"I still think we should wait for the Gonzales book. Hispanic author, all about 'the streets', gritty, powerful. It's right up her alley."

"I disagree. Send this one."

The rep leaned forward onto Jennifer's desk. "And what if instead of a plug it gets a bashing? What if she thinks it's shit?"

Jennifer paused for a moment, then looked him straight in the eyes. Calmly and quietly she said, "What if you're out of a job tomorrow?"

The rep turned and stomped out.

Just as her office door closed, the phone rang.

She reached over the stacks of manuscripts, CDs, and artwork and picked it up. "This is Jennifer," she snapped.

"Jenny, hi, it's Mom."

Not what Jennifer wanted to hear. Not this morning. "Oh, hi, Mom, what's up? Listen, I can't talk long."

"I won't hold you, hon. I got a call from your brother. He's in Africa. Nairobi."

"Africa! Good Lord, what now?"

"I don't know, but it sounds serious. He wants your dad and I to meet him. Actually he wanted you and Jesse to come, too."

Jennifer was amazed. This was a first. "What's the problem?"

"He says..." As she began to speak, the gravity of what her son had said to her minutes ago suddenly resurfaced in her mind. "He says he won't..." My God, she thought to herself, having begun to say the words. She started to well up. Both of her hands were shaking. "He says he won't be seeing..."

"Mom, what is it?"

"He won't be *seeing us* any more. The *family*! Like *forever*, honey!"

"Damn him!" Jennifer snapped. "Will he *ever* grow up? Will that little twit ever figure out that life involves at least a few shreds of consideration and responsibility? And he can't just keep kicking you and Dad around to keep up his little ego trips?"

Alice composed herself. "Honey, don't. Listen, I'm fine. I—"

"Mom, he's full of crap and we both know it! Come on!

It's always the same thing. Little Chrissy has found some 'change the world' scam, and he's going to shove it down all our throats! He's probably joined some screwy religious group."

Despite Jennifer's anger, Alice felt that her daughter was probably right. But she couldn't shake the feeling that it might be something more. The fear and nausea still hovered in her stomach. "We wouldn't ask you to come, hon. We know how busy you are. And Carol's here for Jesse."

"You mean you're *going*? Mom, you can't be serious! To *Africa?*"

"Yes."

"And Dad, too? No way!"

"Yes. Both of us. We're leaving tomorrow."

"But, Mom—"

"Honey, don't worry about us. We'll call in a few days when we get back."

SEVEN

"Just incredible," Sam said, shaking his head and pacing back and forth in front of the Waltrick's massive stone fireplace. "Africa. Of all places!"

"Sam, please!"

"Alice, don't you see what's happening here? It's the same old dance, with a new tune!"

"But we can't be sure of that!"

"Did he say he was in any danger? That he was hurting or threatened in any way?"

"No."

"Right. Of course not. Because he's perfectly *fine,* Alice. He's found some new cause, some crazed goddamned group or New Age 'miracle' or some other totally illogical reason to cause trouble, and he hasn't gotten any *attention* out of you for a while!"

"Sam, it was his voice. He wasn't the usual Christopher."

"What do you mean? What the hell is the usual Christopher?"

"I don't know. I just—"

"Did he sound frightened?"

"No. I think that was part of it. He sounded so...so peaceful and content. As if he'd found everything he'd ever wanted. And he didn't need," The tears began to come, "need *us* any more!"

"What do you mean, peaceful? What did he say, exactly?"

"Something about a special place. A place he wanted us to see, especially *you!* And he talked about a bridge to get there. He said he knew he'd caused us a lot of trouble and he wanted to give us a gift."

"Ah! A gift! A trip to Africa! A little *vacation*! As if we haven't been through enough, for Christ's sake."

"Sam, please!"

"Listen to me, Alice, this is crap. Now you know how much I love you, and you know I love him, too. But this is absolutely crazy! I'm in the middle of a critical executive transition here. I have *got* to be here every minute to get this new organizational structure in place."

Alice stared at her husband, her eyes filling with tears.

"Don't you see what he's doing? Don't you realize that it's time you stopped being his...his way out?"

Alice said nothing.

Sam slammed his palm against the stone mantle. "Damn it, Alice, you *enable* him! You *allow* him to gallivant around the globe and do this, this crazy bullshit to us! I thought he'd grow out of it. I assumed that with a little time he'd come to his senses. But I'm really beginning to doubt this kid. I think as long as you keep this up, as long as you *help* him do this, he's going to stay out of control!"

Alice had begun crying quietly. She turned away from her husband and stared out at their combed lawn and gardens. The rain was falling steadily.

Sam took a deep breath, composed himself, and moved to his wife. He sat on the ottoman in front of her, held her trembling hands, and in a very gentle voice said, "I'm sorry, sweetheart. I love you more than anything on this earth. You know that. And you know I love my son—very much. But for God's sake, honey, *Africa?*"

One year, when a terrible drought hovered over the land, young people came from other countries to help the dying. One was a girl named Alison, but in the village where Cheliese lived she was given the name Ona because she was black, and she was also a beautiful, gentle woman who loved all people, especially the dying children.

She became close to Cheliese. Because of this, and because she was an educated young girl who might know of strange things, the old woman confided in her one day about the dreams. "They have become so strong," she said, "that I must begin writing down the story they are telling me. It is a grand story, but the language that comes to me is not one people will understand. And yet, it is the only way the story can be told."

The young girl seemed unsure about how to advise the old woman, but she said, "Would you like me to bring you writing tools?"

"Yes," Cheliese said.

"But how can you write this story in words that people will understand?"

"I must find a way," the old woman said.

The young girl brought Cheliese paper and pencils and the old woman made a reed binding and satchel. And from that day on, she could be seen carrying the satchel whenever she left the village. She would often remain alone for days in the bush, attempting to write down what she was learning.

Eventually the young girl left Ethiopia, and soon after this, the old woman decided that she, too, must go. She had decided to walk away for good, listen to the dreams, and let them guide her where she should walk. The elders in the village bid her farewell and wished her happiness, though she knew that they believed she had lost her senses and would soon be dead because old women often begin to die when their children and husbands are gone and their lives hold little meaning.

The old woman walked for many days. She ate roots, grubs and berries, and slept under the brilliant stars for many nights. She stopped often to write her story. Eventually the hard ground gave way to grassland and finally to the poverty-stricken outskirts of the city of Nairobi. It was then that something amazing happened, and Cheliese knew she had reached the place the dreams had told her about. She stopped and dreamt and the enormity of what she then experienced confirmed to her that she could not do, alone, what the dreams had asked of her.

Seeking help, she went into the city of Nairobi. Though she despised the smell of disease, the noise, anger and greed she found in the crowded streets, she knew she must wait. She became a pitied old woman, often eating what she could find in trash cans and accepting help from those few compassionate souls who offered. She waited because she felt the dreams required it, and she hoped that from this wretched place, comfort would somehow come to her. But soon the dreams stopped and she felt very old and tired.

It was at this time that two fateful things happened.

She met, once again, the young girl, Ona, who had given her the tools to write. She told the girl of the miracle she had experienced, and soon after this, she became very sick with an old woman's fever.

EIGHT

The flight from Los Angeles International Airport to Nairobi, Kenya takes approximately twenty hours. Even traveling in first class, the trip is grueling. During the initial hours, Sam took notes, talked on the in-flight phone, worked on his laptop, and read project files and business journals. Alice read and crocheted. After dinner and wine, the couple played gin rummy. As night fell, they talked quietly about the instructions Christopher had given to Alice.

"He said to take the Kenya-Jomo Van Service," Alice said, "and check into the Quanteeri Savannah Hotel. He said a room would be reserved and we'd be contacted."

"How soon after we get there?"

"I have no idea. But he did say it would be a woman—a black woman named Ona."

"Did he say anything about who this woman is, or what she is to him?"

Alice shook her head.

"Did he say *anything* about her? How we'd know her? What she looked like? Where she was from?"

"No. I've told you, Sam, all he said was that she was a good and absolutely trustworthy person. He said we could feel completely comfortable going with her and doing whatever she asked of us. And he said she'd take us straight to him."

"Whatever she asks of us," Sam said, chuckling and shaking his head. "God knows what we're in for."

Alice turned toward the window, staring out into the darkness. She remembered the last time she had felt Christopher in her arms. The day he left she'd hugged him tightly, pleading with him to stay. The cold smell of his canvas jacket was still fresh in her nostrils. The feel of his long, curly blond hair clutched in her palm. The tears welling up in his almond colored eyes as he pulled away and turned.

With the image of her son hovering in her mind, she suddenly thought of her voice message to Jane. Would her therapist realize there was a crisis? For nearly a decade their weekly conversations had helped Alice maintain a sense of grounding and hope, and during that time she had come to think of Jane as more of a very close friend and confidante than as her therapist.

She turned back to Sam.

"Sam," she said, "I want you to know that whatever we find, and whatever you feel about Christopher and this whole thing, I understand how hard this is for you. The fact that you're here right now is one of the reasons I love you so much."

Sam smiled weakly. "You're a pain in the rear, you know that?"

Alice felt much better. "I know it. God, I know it."

"But never for yourself. That's the thing, honey. Always for someone else. Always for the kids or me. How the hell do I argue with that?"

Alice, too, managed a smile. She knew now that he understood.

As Sam laid his head back on his seat, the well-being of his son drifted into his mind. What if Chris *were* actually in danger? What if he were involved in some sort of cult or brainwashing activity? Sam had heard those types of things were very common in Africa. He remembered the Jim Jones suicide in Guyana during the late 1970s. And he recalled the television news coverage he'd seen inside a mansion near San Diego. The Heaven's Gate cult whose members thought a spaceship was awaiting them behind the tail of the Hale-Bopp Comet. The mass suicide from drinking a poisoned mix. Bodies lying on bunk beds throughout the house.

He suspected, and was correct, that Alice had also thought of this possibility. Now, as he closed his eyes and listened to the deep, external roar of jet engines, he realized she'd probably thought long and hard about it.

Sam considered contacting the police when they arrived in Nairobi. He decided that might be a possibility, but not immediately. He had to get more facts on Christopher first. He had to know what the boy was involved in, if he was truly in danger, and that he was not somehow breaking the law.

And how should he do that? By first meeting this Ona

person? By questioning her about Chris before agreeing to do anything or go anywhere? Yes, he decided. Then, if he felt the boy was safe and not incriminated in any way, perhaps he would contact the local police or maybe even the U.S. Embassy. With these thoughts in mind, he began to drift off into a restless sleep.

NINE

Jesse Waltrick lay awake on his bed whispering repetitive sounds. On this night, sleep would not come to him. Jesse had no idea why, but then, in many ways he understood very little of what went on around him. For most of his life, Jesse's world had been a very special consciousness of images, smells, sounds, colors, and a kind of cohesive flow of these things in his mind, all of which created feelings.

The expressions on a person's face could bring waves of comfort or discomfort along with accompanying sensations in the pit of his stomach. He had no descriptive words for these feelings and sensations, but he was very good at recognizing them. If the expression was a smile or one of positive excitement, the feelings were good, the kind he liked to feel and hoped for often. If the expressions were of love or tenderness, these brought different feelings, but still the kinds he liked. Other expressions brought opposite feelings, like the few times he had experienced scowls, shouting, or threatening stares. These brought strange, very uncomfortable sensations that Jesse did not like. Sometimes they also brought tears and an uncontrollable reflexive urination.

Jesse was also very much attuned to the space around him. It was a world of colors, varying depths, perspectives, and objects—some soft, some hard, some open, some bright, some dark, some close, and some very wide and distant. Most of these he liked. And, of course, he loved the stars—the sparkling ceiling of lights he would never understand, but which brought him an exciting sense of openness and freedom. Jesse also loved the deep shadows, dappled green patterns, and fiery sunlit yellows created by leafy trees and ferns. His mother and Carol had learned this and filled the Constellation Wing with the greenery of a magical jungle. And finally, Jesse recognized and loved the constant cycle of light and dark, sun and stars, sound and silence. He understood how they came and went and he was very aware that a kind of natural rhythm existed in their cycles. In fact, nearly everything in Jesse's world had merged into a loving, comfortable flow of cycles.

The only exception was words.

For Jesse, words were not part of the general flow of things around him. They, too, created feelings, but their sounds did not hover in his stomach, or pass like waves and rhythmic sensations through his mind. And they were not a part of the colors, smells, or changes in light and dark.

Instead, the combinations of sounds and tones that came from the mouths of those who loved him did something completely different. They instilled a kind of pride and satisfaction in Jesse. Perhaps this was because when he listened carefully to words, he knew that the sounds were not just random or cyclic. They were purposely intended to make him feel certain ways. He was sure this was the case, and in his own way, he viewed himself as a kind of very wise person each time he recognized this.

These may have been the reasons Jesse chattered frequently, most times using strings of words in tones and patterns that he liked. "Mommy," "Daddy," and "Oh boy" were some of his favorites. They never failed to bring good sensations and the music they made when he ran them together produced the most pleasant and wisest feelings he experienced.

On this night, because he sensed that things were not exactly as they always had been, because some change had occurred, or was about to, in the repetitious rhythms of his life, he whispered these very familiar, very comforting sounds to himself. "Mommy and me and my mommy and me and my daddy and mommy and daddy and mommy and me and oh boy oh boy oh boy oh mommy oh boy..."

As he quietly voiced these words, he rolled his head, arched his neck, and smiled. These were the best sounds—the ones he needed now because something was different. Something...

It was the repetition of his favorite sounds and the slow, rhythmic flow of his changing world that finally comforted Jesse and soothed him into letting go of the shadowy leaves and starlight, and passing into a deep, comfortable sleep.

TEN

"Are you joking?"

Mitchell Solomon finished a sip of his Scotch. "Would I joke about being fired by the man himself?"

"Christ! So what now?"

"I don't know. Ever since I walked out of his office I've been going back and forth between elation and panic—'Jesus! I'm actually done with all these greedy, over inflated egos,' then a few seconds later, 'Holy shit! I am officially *un-em-ployed!*'"

Don Mason shook his head. "Hey, it is what it is, and you'll deal with it, right? Think positive." He lifted his glass, offering a toast. "Here's to your newfound freedom. Or demise. Whatever. I'm jealous."

Solomon lifted his glass and the two clinked and sipped. From a small, corner stage a jazz trio had begun a slow, melancholy arrangement and Mason noticed an attractive redhead at a table across the room, looking his way. He smiled and winked. She returned the smile, then turned back to a conversation with her friends.

Solomon stared at the ice in his glass. "I haven't been with it for months."

"Burnt out on the pressure?"

"No, I like the action. Something's… I'm not sure."

"Probably your sense of dignity saying stop all this Waltrick dirty work. Reclaim your soul, young man! Become a frikken teacher!" Both men chuckled and Mason ordered two more scotches. "My treat," he said. "You're going to need it now. How are you fixed for cash?"

"I'm good. After he dropped the axe, Sam finished up with, 'I'll be sure we send you off comfortably.' Not sure what his definition of comfortable is, but I'll find out soon. I've been told to set up a meeting with HR."

"The official send off."

"Right."

"I hear Carson did pretty well. Not sure how much, but he wasn't complaining."

"So what do you think? Look for a job, or enjoy a little R & R first?"

"Hey, that's a no-brainer!"

The drinks arrived and the two toasted again. As Solomon felt the whiskey bite, the muted sounds of cymbal brushes and a gentle flute drifted through the room. He thought back to the odd look on Sam's face just before he'd left. Solomon couldn't figure out what he'd seen flash in the CEO's eyes, but it was something strange and disquieting. As if the two secretly shared some dreadful knowledge or premonition.

"Hey, I know," Mason said, breaking Solomon's trance. "Get yourself a hooker, a little snort and party, party, party!"

ELEVEN

As the 747 began its descent into the Nairobi, Kenya, Jomo International Airport, it crossed above the green carpets of neighboring Uganda, the rugged Ruwenzori Mountain Range, and the vast expanse of Lake Victoria.

Sam looked out the window at craggy peaks rearing out of deep jungle, the glassy blue acres of water, and the broad expanses of the Serengeti just to the south. The flat, broad, snow-covered monolith of Kilimanjaro was also visible. The panorama was breathtaking.

Though he was still furious at Christopher, he'd begun to experience a sense of calm. Perhaps, he thought, it was the incredible view, the vast yellow plains, or the mountains and carpets of jungles that surrounded them. Perhaps it was the simplicity and purity of what stretched thousands of feet below him combined with the now virtually soundless descent of the aircraft. Maybe he was just plain tired. Sam wasn't sure. He only knew that although he had resisted, and he would continue to do so, in some strange way, all of this was beginning to seem right. He felt Alice's hand on his.

He turned toward his wife.

She was smiling gently.

TWELVE

The shuttle ride through the streets of Nairobi was a contrast of modern technology, poverty, and primitive tradition. For Alice, it was analogous to the pixilated color photographs she'd often seen in newspapers and magazines. From a distance things looked smooth, polished, and clean. The downtown skyline was tall, white and matted like a postcard against a bright, blue African sky. But as they entered the city, the perspective became much closer. The pixels became larger, looser, more visible. And this exposed the reality—countless tiny flaws and inconsistencies that were the building blocks of the bigger picture. The filth, poverty, ignorance, and eons of primitive struggle.

She thought Sam probably felt the same, and in the midst of their bumpy ride through the noisy, bustling streets, he confirmed it. "Right," he said, shaking his head as he stared out the window. "A little gift, Christopher. An African vacation for your mother and me."

Alice remained quiet. She would see him soon. God, she thought, she would see her son soon!

The Quanteeri Savannah Hotel was a stark contrast to Nairobi's poverty and squalor. Nineteen stories of polished granite formed its smooth exterior. Its windows were tinted dark and this, along with the gray-blue granite walls and rounded corners, gave the structure a formidable, almost eerie look. From the outside, it seemed to match the geography of the nearby mountains—another towering, magnificent peak—but this one sprung from the tar and smoke of strife and poverty, instead of the pristine carpets of jungle.

Inside, all hint of poverty was erased. Huge palms, thick bushes, and giant leafy plants filled the immense atrium. A trickling stream ran through its center, surrounded by tall savannah grass clumps, rock formations, and trees. Rising the full nineteen stories out of a lush, central oasis was a beveled glass, gold trimmed elevator. Surrounding the elevator and lining the walls of the atrium were restaurants, shops, and a rustic African motif bar called the Silverback Lounge.

The atmosphere was superbly pristine and tropical, and the initial service seemed equally top notch. Obviously made aware of Sam's arrival, the hotel's general manager approached to greet the couple as they stepped from the van. "Good morning," he said, "Mr. and Mrs. Waltrick?"

"Yes," Sam responded.

"Sir and Madame, it is certainly my pleasure to welcome you to our hotel. I am Darrick Onsullent, the general manager."

"Thanks," Sam said extending his hand.

"Please feel free to call on me personally for any of your needs. My staff can arrange tours, visits, or any activity you'd like."

"Thank you," Sam said.

"Though all our guests are special, Mr. and Mrs. Waltrick, we consider you two very important persons. For that reason I would like to invite you to have this evening's dinner as our guests in our finest restaurant, The Rain Forest."

"You're very kind. We'd love to," Alice said, equally impressed.

Onsullent then presented the couple with individual keys to the VIP Lounge and the private health club.

"I'm very appreciative," Sam said, "but I'm also curious. How did you know we were arriving and who we are?"

"We were contacted by your son, sir, Mr. Christopher and his assistant," Onsullent said. "They told us of your high expectations and of your positions of influence in the United States."

"I see. And do you know my son?"

"No sir, I am afraid I do not." He smiled broadly. "But perhaps Mr. Christopher will come and stay with us as well!"

"Yes, perhaps. Thank you."

Immediately following this exchange, the Waltricks' bags were brought to their suite, which Sam and Alice both found to be spacious and exquisite.

The moment they were alone, Sam moved to the window and drew back the drapes. Though not quite as sensational as the aerial view during their descent, this view was also breathtaking. Immediately to their left was a portion of the Nairobi business district. Beyond this and to their right, the savannah stretched away into miles of brown and golden acres dotted with streams and clusters of bush and spindly trees. Far in the distance, the plains gave way to rolling hills, and beyond this a range of mountains loomed in shawls of patchy green jungle.

Alice stepped up beside Sam. He placed his arm around her. Something was growing in him, and in her as well. For some inexplicable reason, a sense of peace was attempting to take root in both of their souls—a quiet, safe feeling that seemed to be drawing them together even more closely than normal.

Sam resisted. He was still holding onto his anger, and he planned to express it to Christopher the moment they were face to face. Alice, too, resisted the encroaching sense of peace, but for her the reasons were different. She was here to rescue her son, to save him from some danger. She could not allow herself to be lulled by the magical beauty of this primitive continent. She knew she must focus clearly and maintain a sense of urgency and momentum until Christopher was safe in her arms.

But the feelings would not be resisted. Without words they told both Sam and Alice that for the moment, for a very brief fraction of time, they should allow the beauty in, allow the mystery and sensuality that was a part of this continent's ancient soul to possess them.

The couple kissed slowly and gently, in a way they had not kissed for many years. They embraced and the meeting of their bodies was alive with an overwhelming sense of warmth and intimacy they had long ago forgotten. They made love and for both it was a fresh, exciting, and deeply spiritual joining of their bodies, hearts, and minds.

They slept naked, side by side.

THIRTEEN

It was 4:00 p.m. when they woke. Sam was famished, so the couple showered and dressed for dinner.

Alice had just stepped into the bathroom to finish her makeup when the phone rang. Sam was leafing through a folder of company reports. He dropped the reports and picked it up immediately. "Hello?"

Alice stepped out of the bathroom.

"Hello," a soft, calm female voice said, "Mr. Waltrick?"

"Yes," Sam said, glancing up quickly and nodding at Alice. She rushed to the bed beside him.

"My name is Ona. I believe Christopher mentioned that I'd be calling?"

Sam felt his temples begin to throb. Suddenly a sinking feeling swept over him. Would this be a *ransom* call? Had some group who knew of Sam's wealth kidnapped Christopher and forced him to make his call to Alice? "Yes, he did," Sam said, holding a controlled, steady tone.

"Let me start by saying that we know how difficult this has been for you and your wife. We realize that."

"We?" Sam said.

"Yes. Christopher and I."

Sam decided that beating around the bush would be foolish. "I want to speak to Christopher. Immediately," he said.

After a pause the voice responded—calm, polite, and intelligent. "And he wants to speak with you, as well. Actually, he wants very much to *see* you. That's why he's asked for my help."

"Let me speak with him. I want to know he's alright."

Again there was a pause, and again the voice came back unperturbed. "I'm afraid he's not here right now, but I—"

"Look," Sam interrupted, feeling the anger begin to take over. "Let's drop the bullshit. Let's at least be up front about this. I left my work and brought my wife half way around the world on the strength of a single damned phone call! And I'm not a man who needs dances or charades. Just lay it on the table and tell me what's going on with my son."

"I know how unnerving this must be, sir, but please believe me when I say that Christopher is perfectly fine and free to do as he chooses. The only reason I'm making this call instead of him, Mr. Waltrick, is because he *asked* me to do so as a favor. It's that simple."

"Fine. Then where is he? How can I see him right now?"

"He's asked me to ask you to please come to where he is."

"Oh, I see, and why's that?"

"Because the gift he would like to give you cannot be brought to you. It is here with him."

Sam could feel himself being maneuvered. "And where exactly is he right now?"

"I'm sorry, but that has to remain a secret. You will understand why when—"

"This is crap!" Sam shouted. "You're manipulating me and you *know* it! You're setting me up for some sort of payoff or extortion. Admit it!"

This time the pause was longer. Finally the voice came again. "Mr. Waltrick, sir, I believe Christopher told your wife that I was a good friend of his, and that I had no other motive than to help you meet. And I believe he said that I could be trusted."

"Right. Sure. And how do I know he said that of his own volition? How do I know you people didn't have a damn gun to his head?"

Alice could see her husband getting progressively more infuriated. Being cornered was something that never worked on Sam Waltrick. No one maneuvered him into a defensive posture. She knew it would be a matter of seconds before he hung up the phone out of sheer reflex. The fear of that caused her to begin trembling.

The voice did not answer Sam's last challenge. He pushed further. "It's simple. I'll be glad to come and meet with Christopher wherever he is, *if* he gets on the phone and I'm sure it's his desire that I do. Not yours or anybody else's."

"Mr. Waltrick, I ask that you just give me a few minutes

to explain. If you then still feel that you're being manipulated, I'll simply hang up."

"And what happens to Christopher?"

"Nothing happens to Christopher. As I told you, I'm only doing this as a favor to him. If you don't feel you can accommodate his wishes, I'll simply tell him that and what he does from that point is his choice."

Sam vacillated. This person sounded sincere. And she kept insisting that none of this was anything other than a simple request on his son's part. Could that be true? Could Christopher have really asked her to do this? Why? Why not talk to him and Alice himself? He could ask them to come to wherever he was. He could still give them this so called gift. Why the third party? He decided to simply ask. "Before you do that, I have one question. If you can answer it reasonably, I'll listen."

"And that is?"

"Why exactly are *you* calling? Why isn't Christopher talking to us directly?"

"He did talk to your wife, Mr. Waltrick."

"But not to me."

"Christopher, himself, will need to answer that. But I can assure you—"

"Go to hell!" Sam shouted. "Have my son call me or don't bother me again!" He slammed down the phone.

Alice was horrified. "God, Sam!" she shouted, "What did you do?"

Sam was furious. His face had become red with rage and he was trembling as he got to his feet and began to stomp around the room. "I called their damn bluff. That's what I did. Sons of bitches! Who the hell do they think they are?"

"What did they say? Can we see Chris?"

"They wouldn't put him on! He's not there. He wants this girl to do it. He's just fine. Well, good! If he's fine then we've got nothing to worry about. He'll call. If it's some sort of extortion or kidnapping plot, they won't give up. They'll call back, Alice, I know they will. Either way, we're fine."

"But Sam, what if they *don't*? What if they *hurt* him?" "What if they... Oh God, Christopher!"

Sam came to her side and took her in his arms. "Listen to me, Alice. Trust me. I know people. I know how things like this are done. I know about bluffs and manipulation. Christopher is fine. He'll—"

Suddenly the phone rang again. Alice dove for it. "Hello!"

"Hello, Mom," came the quiet voice. "It's Chris."

"God, honey! What's going on? Please don't do this to us! Are you okay? Are—"

Sam grabbed the phone. "Christopher!" he snapped, still hovering at the boiling point.

"Hi, Dad."

"What in God's name are you doing? Do you realize the kind of turmoil you are causing? Do you have any idea—*any* idea whatsoever of the kind of grief and pain you've been causing your mother? Have you just gone completely off the deep end, for Christ's sake?"

Silence.

"Christopher! Christopher, answer me!"

Alice reached for the phone. "Sam, please!"

"No," Sam snapped. "I've had it. This is bizarre. We are this boy's *parents*! He owes us the respect of at least providing us with an explanation!"

"Please," Alice pleaded reaching for the phone. Sam waved her off and turned away.

"Dad," Christopher said.

"Yes."

"You're right. I do owe you an explanation."

"You're damn right you do!"

"Okay. I've found a place that's like no other place on earth. It's a place with answers. With incredible knowledge."

"What is this place? What do you mean? A church? A cult?"

"No, Dad. A place in the jungle. A kind of wilderness across a bridge."

"What bridge?"

"An amazing... Look, I want to share this place with you and Mom."

"How do we get to you?"

"Dad, listen to me. I know you're not going to believe this but, the jungle on the other side of this bridge is, well, there's something spiritual that happens there, something..."

Sam shook his head. "Jesus Christ. Here we go again!"

"Dad, listen to me. I know what you think, but I'm only going to say this one time. I mean it. I'm going to cross this bridge soon, and stay on the other side. I won't be coming back, ever. I've made that decision. Before I do that, I wanted you and Mom to understand this place, what happens there. And I wanted to make things right between us. I've wanted that since I left. I love you…and I'm asking that you trust me just once more in your life. This one last favor is all I will ever ask of you and Mom again, as long as I live."

This caught Sam by surprise. His first thought was to stop Christopher in his tracks and tell him that no one, not even his son, issued ultimatums to Sam Waltrick. But the boy sounded dead serious. Was it a bluff? Would they never hear from him again after this phone call, if Sam didn't capitulate? And if that were the case, could Sam live with that? And face his wife? Could he live with the knowledge that he had actually turned away from his son at the most critical time in their relationship? And would Alice ever forgive him? He knew how much she loved him and how dedicated she was to supporting his beliefs. But this? Although it was excruciating for him, the man who never caved in during negotiations said, "Where is this place?"

"I can't tell you that."

"What? Why can't you tell us, damn it?"

"Because I don't know myself."

Sam shook his head again. He was on the verge of exploding.

But this time, before he could act on his frustration, Alice surprised him. She flew across the bed and yanked the phone from his hand. "*No!*" she shouted, tears suddenly streaming from her eyes. "No, Sam! Not this time! This is our *son*! Our *flesh and blood*! This is *my* responsibility. I don't care what he wants, I don't care where he is. I don't care what he's done! We are going to see him! *I'm* going to see him! *I* am going to see him. If you don't want to come, go home! Do you hear me? *Go home*!"

Sam stood dumbfounded at the edge of the bed.

After a long pause, Alice lifted the phone to her ear. "Christopher," she said, still looking directly at Sam. "You tell me what to do and where to go. I'll come right now, sweetheart."

During her time of sickness, Cheliese experienced little that she would remember later. A wind of images swept through her mind, but they were not like the dreams she had experienced for so many years. The dreams of her fever had no meaning or language. They were clouded and chaotic, and brought with them a warm, nauseating discomfort that seemed to envelop the old woman and force her deeper and deeper into a kind of darkness she had never before experienced.

Eventually the darkness seemed to close in and the hot, suffocating blackness continued to press on her chest, making it more and more difficult to breathe. She struggled to free herself, but could not. The pressure increased, and finally, not only did the darkness stop the air from entering her chest, it began to draw the breath from her mouth.

Though she remained unconscious, Cheliese sensed she was nearing her time of passing and that her story would go untold. At first this saddened her, but it was out of this darkness, in what had seemed like the final moments of her life, that one of the last pieces of her puzzle appeared. Slowly, she felt the darkness begin to subside. Her breath began to rise in her chest, and a wonderful cool feeling of release grew in her mind and body. Somehow she had begun rising, ascending toward light, shedding the hot weight of her death.

And when she finally found the strength to open her eyes, she saw a face. At first she was confused because it was a young face with pale skin and yellow hair. No special knowledge gleamed in the bright almond eyes, no reasons or answers. But soon she realized there was something important in the brilliance and colors she now saw before her. The luminous brown orbs and pale skin did have meaning. Yes! Something about this face had been present in her dreams! Aware that the eyes she was now looking into knew nothing of her journey, the old woman suddenly realized they gleamed with a kind of power.

They were not the final piece of her puzzle.

They were not the eyes she still hoped to see, and yet…

FOURTEEN

At 8:30 the next morning, Sam and Alice walked out of their hotel and turned left onto Diamond Day Boulevard. Alice held a piece of hotel notepaper. She looked down at it briefly and said, "Three blocks this way, to Aloon."

Sam said nothing. The couple walked the three blocks in silence. They turned left. After continuing for two more blocks, they found themselves in what seemed to be a coffee house district. Most of the buildings were old and rustic, and there were quite a few tourists and young people on the street. Most paid little or no attention to Sam and Alice as they moved past the couple, engrossed in their own conversations. A few minutes later, the couple rounded a corner and saw a small, hand painted sign that read simply, "Noosilos Embers."

They stepped into a small restaurant and bar.

The motif was dark, rustic, and African. The tables were bamboo and rattan. Heavy smoke hung in the still air with a very strong tobacco aroma. Across the room a jazz trio played what Sam thought was a nearly unrecognizable version of Dave Brubeck's "Take Five." Zulu clothing, headdresses, and spears hung on one wall. Decorative tablecloths and turtle shell candles sat on each table. Animal skins and beaded curtains acted as dividers in doorways, separating different areas of the club.

Sam and Alice found a small table and sat down. When the waiter arrived, Sam ordered coffee and juice. Alice ordered tea. As the waiter took the order, Alice brought out a second piece of hotel notepaper from her purse. On it, at Christopher's instruction, she had written the words "Eden Journey." She turned to the waiter. "Maybe you can help me," she said. "My son told me that if I came here, I should inquire about this." She held up the piece of paper.

The waiter smiled. "Yes," he said, "I'm aware of this journey. A representative will be here soon. Would you like to meet her?"

"Yes," Alice replied.

Moments later the drinks arrived, and twenty minutes after this a young, beautiful black woman approached their table. She was about Christopher's age, and very thin with high, round cheeks and short hair cropped close to her head. She wore sandals, jeans, and a T-shirt. With a polite smile and an extended hand she said, "Hello. My name is Ona."

"Hello," Sam said. "Our son, Christopher?"

"Yes," Ona said politely, nodding. "I'd be happy to take you to your son. Christopher has been very anxious to see you both. Would you like to leave now?"

"Yes," Alice said. She and Sam finished their drinks and got to their feet.

The woman led them under a thin yellow curtain, down a hallway, and out a back door. A white van was parked in the alley beside the building. Sam noticed that it had no side windows. He and Alice stepped in through the sliding side door. Their guide slid it closed and took the driver's seat. The van started immediately and pulled away slowly.

As they made a right turn toward what Sam thought was the eastern part of the city, he tried to peek through two short curtains blocking off the front section of the van. The rear windows had been covered with wood. Both Sam and Alice realized that they would have no idea where they were going. Every instinct in Sam's body told him that he and his wife were in danger and he should stop the van immediately, but he suppressed the urge. Instead, he decided to try to keep some sort of mental bearing by glancing at his watch and counting the minutes between turns, remembering the direction each time and the number of them, the types of roads they traveled, and whatever other characteristics of the trip that might help them to retrace their path.

Glancing down at his watch he noted the time was 9:13. He looked over at Alice and, for just a moment, was surprised to see her eyelids drooping, as if she were about to slip off into a nap. Odd time to feel like napping, he thought. His next thought brought a frightening possibility. Was something wrong? There was no way his wife should be sleepy! Again the flight instinct rose up in him. Following this wave of fear, he had only enough time to think to himself, "The drinks! We've both been... God!"

FIFTEEN

In San Francisco, California it was early Sunday morning. Jennifer was seated at her computer, sipping coffee in her pajamas. She had just typed the words "African religious cults" into an online search engine. Surprisingly, she got nearly 150,000 results. Many appeared to be recruitment sites, but a few provided information about the nature of cults, the ultimate control they can have and how they manage to exist. At one site she read:

> The people who are drawn to cults vary in many respects. Many are loners or outsiders who have a difficult time fitting into society. Those who have recently experienced a life crisis are also very susceptible to the promise of heightened revelation through cults. Alcoholics or drug addicts who have reached the "bottom of the barrel," people in the midst of divorce, or those who have lost a loved one fall into this same category. Also prime targets are the gullible, the

> uneducated, and those who have deep personal needs they feel cannot be met by society.

None of these profiles fit her family. Maybe Christopher, as a loner or outsider, but definitely not her father or mother.

After checking out several more sites, most of which were of questionable credibility or what she considered downright creepy, she came across an article about a cult that called itself the "Sacred Journey." The article appeared to be an academic research paper, and, surprisingly, a botanist with very impressive credentials had written it.

As she began to scan it, Jennifer quickly discovered why a botanist had written a paper on cults. According to him, the Sacred Journey cult had been spawned when founding members were exposed to something called Spider Eye spores. The Spider Eye, she discovered, was a rare, orchid-like flower found only in a few remote areas of Africa. The name had been derived from clusters of eight dots, or "Spider Eye" markings on each of its four large petals.

According to the article, at certain times of the year, slight vibrations or even a gentle breeze could cause the Spider Eye flower to release a dusting of spores that had potent hallucinogenic qualities. For many years, the effects of the spoors had caused those who experienced them to believe they had witnessed profound spiritual events. Some spoke of talking to God, and others spoke of visiting Heaven and Hell. Jennifer read on and found that as the Sacred Journey cult had grown, its members made pilgrimages from distant areas of Africa to visit the places where these "miracles" would occur.

The article went on to say that in recent years, the Spider Eye flowers had been harvested for both scientific and illicit uses. Studies were being conducted by several prominent universities to find possible psychological uses for the spores, but African criminals had also used their effects to bilk gullible individuals—most often Europeans and Americans.

She noted that one of the places where the Spider Eye grew abundantly was east of Nairobi in a remote mountain range bordering Lake Victoria.

She checked out several other sites and found information on various other cults, including their philosophies, histories, and even their leaders' names and member lists. Just as she was about to check another, the phone rang. It was her new boyfriend, Aaron.

"Lunch?" he said. "It's a good day for a Carlisle's salad."

Jennifer thought about it. "Sounds great," she said. "At noon?"

"See you then."

Carlisle's was a small, eclectic hillside restaurant with a panoramic view of the Golden Gate Bridge and a health-conscious, seafood and salad menu. Aaron chose boiled shrimp and Jennifer decided on Ahi tuna.

"You seem distracted," Aaron said, as they waited for their food to arrive.

Jennifer thought about confiding in Aaron, but stopped herself. It was too soon, she decided. She liked this thin, rugged guy a lot. Despite the short, Marine-style crew cut, a remnant of his military days, and cheeks left pitted from what must have been a severe case of teenage acne, she found him sensually magnetic. He was also a self-confident, intelligent, no-nonsense man who owned his own financial consulting business. How would a man with such promising upside potential take to learning that the parents of the girl he had just begun dating had gone off the deep end? No, Jennifer decided, not yet. "I guess I am a little distracted," she finally said. "Work was a bear this week and a few things are going on in my family."

"Nothing too bad, I hope."

"No, not really. Just a younger brother who somehow always manages to stir up trouble and two...well, just two *parents*."

"I'm sorry. Anything I can do?"

Jennifer smiled. "You're doing it," she said.

SIXTEEN

At the same moment, half a state away, Carol Drey sat with Jesse under the bright, open ceiling of the Constellation Wing. Rows of high, wispy clouds drifted above them and the diffused sunlight projected soft, dappled patterns through the palms and fichus.

Jesse had just finished a thirty-minute session with his new physical therapist. Physical therapy was something he didn't care much for and the new program was more demanding than any he had tried in the past. It involved an aggressive regimen of stretches, twists, and other coordination exercises that often frustrated the boy and always wore him out. But it was working. Carol had been noting marked improvements in his flexibility and balance. He was steadier on his feet, and his extremities were less rigid and more dexterous.

Having completed the session he was now relaxed on the huge afghan Alice had made for him, spread over a beanbag chair. Lightly stroking his hair, Carol could hear him whispering to himself as he drifted toward a nap. Carol, too, was feeling drowsy. Her thoughts moved to Sam, Alice, and the boy she held in her arms.

On the verge of sleep, she recalled the events that had brought her to this place in her life. She remembered the day she and Alice had met as freshmen roommates in college, how they had become great friends immediately and how their relationship had grown deep and strong during those years of personal awakening: cramming for finals, summer adventures, and the often-crazed doings of their sorority.

After graduation they had stayed in touch, even taking a few girls-only vacations together to Mexico and the Caribbean. It was on the Caribbean trip that Carol had met Matt Garwick, a heart surgeon. Alice met Sam shortly after this and the four had married, settling into their personal and professional lives as very close friends.

And for a time, everything was perfect.

When both women were in their thirties, however, the perfection they enjoyed was suddenly swept away. Matt was struck with brain cancer. He was gone in two months. Carol remembered telling Alice that the disease had come like a flash flood or tornado. She'd felt she had no chance to do anything but hang on and pray desperately for her own sanity as her husband quickly lost his ability to communicate, withered horribly before her eyes, and was wrenched away from her virtually overnight.

At that same time, Alice was about to give birth to Jesse. Knowing that Carol had become extremely depressed and at one point even suicidal, Alice had insisted that her friend come and stay with her and Sam for a while. The change would do her good, Alice had reasoned, and besides, she'd said she would need help with her new baby. Carol remembered Alice's amazement and delight when she accepted.

Then came the birth.

Jesse.

Beautiful, chubby, eight-pound-nine-ounce Jesse. Thick blond hair, large almond colored eyes, and a smile that over the next four years made every new mother in Hidden Valley sick with envy.

How handsome and perfect he'd been. How happy and active and intelligent...in the beginning.

Returning to the present, she listened to the breathing of the young man sleeping in her arms. As she closed her eyes, she held him even closer to her body.

SEVENTEEN

Sam woke up lying naked in the deep, wet grass of a small jungle clearing. He swung around and saw Alice kneeling beside him looking up. She, like Sam, was naked.

Directly above the couple, a dense canopy of leaves and branches spread across the sky covering all but a few small patches of bright blue. On all sides they were surrounded by towering trees, thick vines, and walls of huge leaves and tendrils. There were no signs of civilization, but Alice noticed what seemed to be a natural, tunnel-like opening nearby in the wall of leaves.

"What the hell?" Sam blurted out, looking first at his naked body, and then at his surroundings. "Holy God!"

He leapt to his feet.

Alice stood up slowly.

"Christ, what in God's name? They've *undressed us*! *Both of us!*" Turning his hands over, he saw that even his rings had been removed. He looked at Alice. Her hands were also bare. "Alice, are you—"

"Sam, I'm okay. There's a reason," she said, gazing up at the lush surrounding jungle. "I think it's... My God, this place! This amazing place!"

With no other seeming options, the couple started moving toward the opening in the vegetation. They found that it was an entrance into a dense covering of leaves and vines that curved away, leading downhill. Hand in hand they started forward.

As they approached the first curve, the path began to descend at a steeper angle. Stones jutted from the earth, creating shallow, natural steps. As they descended, their surroundings became cooler and darker, lit mostly by the few blades of light that sliced through openings between the leaves and branches. Despite the deepening shade, the couple made their way safely. The earth and rough, damp stones gripped the soles of their feet. The fresh smells and wetness of the dense vegetation filled their senses. Then, ahead of, and below them, a brilliant area of grass appeared, and they heard something.

Far in the distance. The sound of rushing water.

They moved out of the shade into a small, sunlit meadow. On all sides but one they were once again surrounded by jungle. To their right, however, was something odd. At first it appeared to be a huge, tangled cluster of vines and branches bunched around a few splintered tree trunks. But a closer look revealed that it was something else.

"A bridge!" Alice said. "A bridge! Sam, he's close! *God, he's here!*"

They started toward it. The sound of the rushing water, though still distant, seemed to heighten and echo.

At the base of the structure they were able to look over the edge of the cliff. Its black granite wall descended hundreds of feet below them, creating a sheer vertical drop. The gap from one side of the gorge to the other appeared to be only about thirty feet and the bridge was the only way across.

It was a completely natural structure. Several huge old trees had fallen across the gorge creating its base. Their weathered and mossy trunks told Sam that they had been in this same position for many years. The tangles of vines and branches that sprouted from these and surrounding trees had interwoven over the years adding to the bridge's natural structure. Vines along the sides of the structure had been pulled down horizontally as other trees had fallen over and formed what gave the appearance of grips and handrails.

The couple looked around, then into each other's eyes.

Something strange was rising up in the motion of the trees, the smells and colors, and a light wind. Both suddenly experienced a lightheaded, almost out-of-body sensation.

"What is it?" Alice asked.

"I'm not sure," Sam said, still looking around. "I have no idea."

The couple realized that at this point questioning anything about this experience was useless. They were here. They had been brought and left here. They had been stripped of all connection to their civilized world. They were two naked human beings in the middle of a natural wilderness, and it seemed that any harm they might have experienced would already have taken place.

Their journey had begun to unfold as they were told it would. In front of them stood what their son had talked about—a bridge to a special place.

Both stepped forward.

EIGHTEEN

Sam placed his foot carefully on the huge, ancient log base and stepped up. Alice came just behind him. Holding her hand, he helped her up. The breeze picked up slightly, thick with cool, natural smells. They stepped forward slowly. Though the bridge appeared to be very old, it felt rock solid. As they inched forward, they felt no bend, no sway. Not the slightest bit of roll. Still, they went very slowly using the branches and vines as rails to steady themselves and provide balance.

At one point, they stopped and attempted to look down through the tangle of vegetation. Far below them, what Sam guessed to be many hundreds of feet, a small opening in the vegetation revealed a glimpse of a white mist. It was so distant and such a small opening, neither could be sure, but it seemed to be a torrent of water rushing through the gorge, tumbling down toward a great expanse of green plain just off to their right. The height was dizzying but the view of that plain was like nothing either had ever seen. Sam took

Alice's arm and pulled her in close to him. "My God," he said. "Look at that."

The two stood for several minutes simply gazing out at the expanse before them. Sam felt they were nowhere near Nairobi. The dry savannahs they had seen only the day before were nowhere in sight. How far had they come? How long had they slept? Where exactly in the name of God was this incredibly beautiful place? And, of course, the biggest question, how did all this connect to their son?

The odd feelings rose again in both, and slowly intensified as they continued forward. For an instant, Sam's consciousness seemed to flip. He found himself swept into a childhood flashback. Suddenly he was standing beside his grandmother at an old white stove. She was boiling a chicken in a large pot to remove its feathers. Sam looked up past her flowered skirt and apron. From under her arm, as she stirred, he saw the bony chicken feet sticking up in the steam as if to pinch. The smell was repulsive, but his grandmother didn't seem to mind or notice it. She smiled down at him lovingly. The vision unfolded in Sam's mind in great detail and over what felt like a very long period of time—countless years. Then, suddenly, he flipped back and realized it had happened in an instant.

Alice was gripped by a similar moment. She found herself seated in the back of her father's old Ford. Beside her were a picnic basket and a stack of jackets. The car radio was playing a baseball game. Rain spattered against the side rear window just above her. As she looked up at it, she began to smile, picturing herself seated in the basket, floating away from a grassy knoll, waving back at her parents. Like Sam's flashback, Alice's seemed to unfold slowly, until she suddenly realized she was back, and it had lasted only a fraction of a second. Alice wasn't sure what was happening. She was sure, however, that these feelings were being brought on by more than simply a change in their surroundings. "There's something here, Sam," she said. "I'm not sure what's happening, but I think Christopher was right!"

The lightheadedness persisted, along with strange sensations that seemed to somehow be affecting time, or the way they perceived it. Sam stopped for a moment, struggling to grasp the enormity of the experience. He suddenly felt as if he had been held still in that spot for an enormous period of time. But the moment quickly passed and he realized he'd taken a single step and was now looking down at his naked foot on the moss-covered log in front him.

They continued to inch forward, arm in arm, taking each step with great care. A few minutes later they reached the far side. Together, they stepped off the log onto a thick bed of wet grass.

Ahead was a low, natural archway under a canopy of towering foliage. As they bent and walked under it, a momentary wave of bizarre sounds and confusion swept over them. Sam heard a pleading whine and then urgent voices somewhere in the distance. He wheeled around just as Alice cried out thinking a pair of wet hands were lifting her—a baby, naked and frightened—toward a light. As these visions gripped Sam and Alice, both clenched as if falling on the initial drop of a huge roller-coaster, and held on for what seemed like the passing of lifetimes. But an instant later the visions released them and they were unsure what had actually happened.

They pushed forward.

Although the jungle they now entered appeared to be completely overgrown and untouched by human presence, as they continued to make headway they kept finding partial openings—suggestions of paths through the huge ferns and thick, leafy foliage. It seemed there was always a way to continue forward. And though neither Sam nor Alice were conscious of it as they inched through the dense walls of leaves and tendrils, in addition to the bizarre sensations, physical changes seemed to be taking place in both of them as well. The first indication was a kind of subtle comfort they both felt as they moved through the jungle. It wasn't easy going by any means, but it took just a little less effort to move through the bush than it should have. They continued on, unaware that the muscles in their legs did not begin to ache as they should have for two middle-aged people moving through this kind of terrain over an extended period of time. Passing through and under the leaves, pushing open the branches and vines also became strangely different. Rather than a strenuous and awkward activity, it began to take on a kind of ease and cadence. It felt to them as if a rhythm had come into their motion and it had begun to aide in their journey. This sense of comfort and ease of movement remained with the Waltricks, though still unnoticed for several minutes. Then it began to intensify.

The waves of lightheadedness and confusion slowly gave way to a sense of mental clarity. Both Sam and Alice felt as if they were awakening out of a very long sleep. They were becoming inexplicably wide-eyed, refreshed, and more exhilarated than they had ever felt in their lives. At the same time, their senses seemed to have suddenly come alive, leaving them finely attuned to the world around them, and a kind of forward momentum entered their cadence. Though they didn't yet fully realize why, both seemed to be leaning forward very slightly as they moved, almost as if using their weight to propel them just a little faster. This leaning posture seemed to fit comfortably with the rhythmic motion of their bodies passing through the foliage.

And now they began to realize what was happening to them, but in an oddly acceptable way. The reason was simple. Just as changes had been taking place in their bodies, changes had also been taking place in their minds. And the two processes were unfolding in perfect unison.

The surrounding jungle seemed to compliment or fit with this new awareness and their way of moving, almost as if becoming an immense, willing participant in the graceful motions they were a part of. As the minutes passed, the vines parted with more and more ease and the huge leaves were swept aside, arching away with less and less effort. Snake-like paths through the ferns and grass seemed to actually move underfoot as if they themselves were somehow alive.

It was shortly after this that deep in the recesses of their minds they began to sense their journey was nearly complete.

When the couple finally reached a clearing, they stopped, squatted and looked at each other. Neither was the least bit taken aback by what they saw—small golden brown eyes sunk deep under heavy brows, thick wrinkled skin, wide, powerful bodies.

NINETEEN

Alice blinked several times and looked straight up into the canopy of leaves and branches overhead. Though it did not seem particularly amazing to her, she heard the feet of birds moving and clutching the branches nearly fifty feet above her. She also heard the fluttering leaves lightly brush each other's wet skins. She knew they were wet by the slightly squeaky sound they made and the thick, fresh scents they released with each touch. She heard and followed the sound of the breeze as it swept from the deep grass and circled through the trees.

Soon she began to sense something like a very quiet sound or slight vibration. For a moment she stopped, cocked her head and wondered what it might be. Then, in some primitive way, she realized it was the universal sound of something wonderful—the subtle, permeating resonance of all earthly movement—the constant, gentle, almost indistinguishable voices of the trees and plants and grass as they swayed in the breeze and slowly, very slowly, grew and changed and aged.

Sam, too, began to sense these things. He, too, felt a great, soothing motion and comfort now enveloping him and Alice. It was simple and exquisite, and like the voices and movements of all things in concert, it was everywhere—the crisp, vibrant scent of the undersides of leaves; the weightless and pungent flight of spores and pollens; the arching motions of birds; the skittering waves of ants; the snakes sliding through the grass and leaves—a mixture of sounds and smells and aging things carried on the wind into an exhilarating presence that permeated all things.

Their golden eyes found each other's. They stared in silence. Only the slightest connection, a single thread to what they had been in another world, remained in their minds—that faster and more complex world in which they sensed all that they were now experiencing had been dulled by words, numbers, pressures, ambitions, complex human thoughts and needs—a completely different kind of consciousness.

They stood up and walked away into the deep grass and thick underbrush. They traveled together for miles, luxuriating in the smells and touches, the tastes of leaves and the skins and bodies of plants. They watched other animals—birds soaring past overhead, mammals slipping through the deep vegetation. They viewed armies of busy insects and delicate spiders carefully tapping their silken strands into place. And with each encounter Sam and Alice became increasingly aware of the same things: a stunning harmony of life; a great, soothing, all-encompassing motion; trillions of living things, held and interwoven with a precision and elegance beyond all comprehension, into a single living entity of life.

TWENTY

As the day unfolded the couple traveled together to many parts of their new world. With each discovery came new revelations, nurtured by their new awareness.

Then a scent came to their nostrils, and moments later a sound—breathing, feet touching deep grass, sinking in the muddy ground. Both stopped and looked toward the dense jungle from where the sounds and smells drifted on the breeze. A shape appeared, moving out from the shadows. A similar shape, young, proud, and strong.

Their eyes met and held.

They had no words, but needed none.

They knew him at once.

For the first time in three years, Sam and Alice faced their son, Christopher. They rushed to him and began to touch and smell, to feel his closeness, and take in the wonderful odors of his hair and flesh.

The group of three traveled together through the forest for hours and as the day finally became red and shadows lengthened on the ferns and meadows, breezes rose up. The nocturnal insects and animals began to wake and move about. The shadows coalesced into dusk and eventually the only remaining light was from the stars—billions of jeweled points of light in the cool, black ceiling rotating above them.

They sat together in a clearing of ferns and grasses.

They languished in the darkness and each other's sounds, smells, and presence. Finally, their eyes caught sight of something in the distance—a kind of light—a glow that seemed to be drawing them, urging them back to a special place. They moved through the forest to a cluster of vines, a fallen log, a bridge and the sound of water.

They crossed slowly in the black, sparkling night.

Becoming tired and confused they reached the other side and huddled together. As their minds hovered between wakefulness and unconsciousness, between humanity and the simian world, they became more and more aware of the thread of humanity that each harbored. This caused waves of intense and bizarre feelings in each of them. Somehow there was good in the thread—a connection to something else they were a profound part of. But, there was also a sadness in the connection. A knowledge that with its complexity would come a great dulling and insulation from what they had just experienced.

As they struggled with these thoughts, they lost consciousness.

TWENTY-ONE

When Sam and Alice awoke they were lying side by side in brilliant sunlight on thatched mats. Each was covered with a brightly colored cloth. Christopher was lying beside them.

Sam stirred and looked up at Alice.

She had awakened and was staring at Christopher.

Sam, too, looked at his son.

Christopher opened his eyes and smiled.

"My God," Sam said. "*My God!*"

TWENTY-TWO

A woman stood at the edge of the clearing. She was a small, very old woman who wore bright metal rings and the colorful cloths of her Ethiopian heritage. One of her arms rested on a woven reed satchel slung across her body. It was decorated with clusters of large, brightly colored beads, and Sam noticed that it contained a heavy object. She smiled bashfully. When Sam, Alice and Christopher looked her way and returned the smile, she leaned forward with a slight bow. She made no attempt to speak, but simply stood in a patch of bright sunlight beneath a towering wall of trees and vines, watching Sam, Alice and Christopher intently. Christopher explained that he believed she and Ona were the only other people in the world who knew of the place they had just experienced.

"Why you, and us?" Sam asked, his mind still dazed and floating in a kind of surreal consciousness from the experience.

"I'm not sure," Christopher responded. "I was working at a free clinic in Nakuru. We treated Cheliese, the old woman, for Dolken's fever, a hyper strain of pneumonia. We almost lost her. She was ranting and delirious for a week. Ona came in every day and sat with her.

"One night late, a few days after the two left the clinic, I was locking up and found Cheliese standing out back in the courtyard. She started gesturing to the satchel she carries and rambling on, acting out some story, waving her arms and dancing. She speaks mostly Swahili, but I was able to fill in some of the blanks.

"Then I realized Ona was standing there, too. Cheliese started shaking her head, talking to Ona and pointing at me insisting on something. Ona pleaded with me to at least visit this special place, and, well..."

Sam looked at the woman, then turned back to his son. He smiled and hugged the boy tightly, a sudden uncontrollable flood of tears welling up in his eyes.

Alice watched, also overcome with emotion. Like Sam she was still dazed, as if in a kind of half-dream. But concern for her son was growing in her mind. "But, Chris, to leave everything?" she finally said. "Your father and me? Your family?"

"You saw, Mom. You both experienced it. You know now."

Sam tried to focus and clear his head. He could not deny that what he had just experienced would change his life forever. His entire value system had been shattered. And the great sadness that had overshadowed his and his wife's life for so many years now seemed insignificant.

But suddenly his demeanor changed. "Wait," he said.

"Before we do anything—any of us—let's talk about this. What exactly *did* we experience? I mean, my God, it was incredible—a revelation like...but was it real?"

"Dad, come on, now. You—"

"No. Think about it. We drink something and we're put to sleep. We're stripped naked, we cross this...this bridge in the middle of a jungle clearing and suddenly we revert back to... Good God! What if it's some sort of trick? Some form of mass hypnosis, hallucinations, or something? I had some bizarre, out-of-body sensations and something like flashbacks at first. I *still* feel odd."

"Me, too," Alice said.

"What if there's something out there that causes delirium? We've heard of stranger things. Suppose—"

"Dad," Christopher interrupted, "think about it. What did you learn in there?"

Sam stopped and thought. He spoke slowly. "Somewhere, back at the source of our origin, we took this wrong turn away from the most amazing and precious part of our existence in the natural world, and—"

"God?"

"I don't know. But we paid a price."

"Exactly. As we gained one kind of knowledge and intelligence, we slowly lost another."

Alice thought about this and suddenly a revelation came to her. "You're exactly right, Chris! What we just experienced wasn't a *lack* of intelligence, but a different *kind* of intelligence!"

Sam smiled. "My God, that's the amazing thing! It was a step into *true* intelligence—an understanding of life and the world based on our most primitive senses. The only way it *can* be understood. *The only way it can be understood! Of course!* You don't talk to, sing, or write about God. You *experience* God!"

"But there are still questions," Christopher said.

"What?"

"For one, why this place? Can you rationalize it? Explain it?"

Sam and Alice both remained silent.

"I think there's more to the story. And if I go back, maybe over time I can understand it."

Sam thought about this. "Chris," he said finally, "we're products of a modern society. Like it or not, we're intellectual animals, and that's the barrier. I have no idea why or how this place exists, but somehow I knew in there that I could only go so far."

"And why does it even matter?" Alice added. "Why not just let it go and be at peace with the truths you've discovered? It's enough!"

Christopher got to his feet. "Not for me," he said, and then nodded toward the old woman, "and definitely not for her."

Sam and Alice turned toward the old woman standing quietly at the tree line. Her black, deeply wrinkled face glistened in the sunlight. Her eyes were bloodshot and yellowed with age, but gleaming with anticipation. "She's searching for something, maybe an answer," Christopher continued, "and she's convinced we can help her find it. And I believe she's right. I don't think it's a coincidence that the three of us are here."

After a long moment of silence Sam turned to Alice. "If that's true, how about us? What do *we* do now?"

Alice was torn. What she had experienced drew her powerfully, just as she knew it drew Sam and Christopher. Nothing else seemed even remotely as important anymore—*almost* nothing else.

She turned to Sam. "We have to tell Jennifer and Carol," she said.

TWENTY-THREE

The trip back to their hotel was as simple as their journey to the bridge—a sedative drink, immediate sleep, and an awakening in a van in downtown Nairobi. Christopher had gone to his apartment.

Sam and Alice had not decided what would be best for them or their family. Nor had they decided what to do about the old woman. They showered, had dinner, and returned to their room.

Later that night, as Alice slept, Sam stepped out onto the balcony. He sat under the stars and attempted to gain a sense of direction. Should he and Alice stay? Bring the rest of their family? Try to help the old woman finish her "story"? To each of these questions, there seemed to be no good answer. And then there were the biggest questions of all. What exactly was this incredible, surreal place? This place that could not possibly exist! *Why* and *how* did it exist? And was there really some predestined purpose behind their visit here?

It was two in the morning when Sam finally slipped into bed beside his sleeping wife and closed his eyes. For some time, the questions persisted. Just as he was finally drifting off to sleep, he made the assumption that he would never know.

TWENTY-FOUR

He was back. Across the bridge. The incredible sense of harmony and balance swept him into its warm, graceful, motion. As he looked up into the jungle canopy, strangely beautiful oval and rectangular shapes of light began to drift down. At first they blended into a warm and brilliant stream of images, but soon they intensified and grew into a powerful flow of light and energy. The flow became wider, deeper, and more and more powerful until its blinding passage of shapes poured out of all things in torrents, like a vast, blazing ocean.

At first Sam was frightened. Undulating in the shapes, like fragmented images from dreams, he saw waves of light on all sides, above and below, swirls of brilliant eddies and splashes leaping out from the central flow. Some curled into their own gleaming vortexes, sparked brilliantly for a moment, and then were swept back into the stream and carried on their way. Others poured on toward eternity.

And he began to notice something.

The flow had a kind of cadence that seemed to keep it purposely moving at varying speeds. That meant something, he was sure, but he couldn't quite grasp what. Like currents in a stream, some images rushed quickly forward while others moved slower, less directly. Some swirled up and around him and others drifted straight past him. But the one thing they all had in common was that they were a part of a greater single flow, and all were carried by its momentum in the same direction—toward eternity.

Sam felt positive that some important truth was apparent in what he was witnessing, some message, but he was behind a filter or curtain of some kind, and though it seemed virtually transparent, he couldn't quite seem to focus clearly on what was on the other side.

Then, suddenly, he saw something familiar in the images, the way they circled and flowed. Their primitive, but cohesive curves and lines. Something he knew he'd experienced. Something terrible and frightening!

Though the answers appeared to be right in front of him, he couldn't quite grasp them. He was on the verge of crying out, when he realized someone else was there, close by. It was not Alice, but possibly Christopher. No. It was someone else. He couldn't make out whom. It was a naked male, slim in stature, very young. Amazingly this person seemed to fit perfectly into Sam's vision. He sat naked with his back to Sam, his arms moving gracefully in wide circular motions. He appeared mesmerized by the motion of the images swirling around him. And they seemed to be telling him something. He seemed to be learning, understanding what Sam could not quite bring to the surface. He reached out with long, slender arms toward the flow of images, accepting their knowledge, and they seemed to somehow permeate and fill his being.

Arching his back and neck, he turned slightly. His head rolled back and…

Sam was stunned. It was Jesse!

And the images! *Of course!* Scribbled shapes on a bedroom wall nearly fifteen years earlier. The primitive, crayon-colored lines that seemed to have had an order—a meaning of some sort. The waving arms.

That horrible night he and Alice had lost their son!

Sam gasped as the light suddenly drew back, and what remained was his fragile, disabled boy, now transformed, in a jungle wilderness. At first, Sam was fearful and wanted to call out, but his fear was swept away almost immediately. Jesse, the son who had suffered such indignities and terrible restrictions in his own world, moved about in this world so easily and comfortably it filled Sam with a sense of joy and well-being.

Other shapes appeared, what Sam thought were simians, and Jesse walked among them comfortably, with an ease that seemed perfectly natural—as if he'd been a part of this world all along. He even seemed to be communicating in some primitive way. It was almost as if…

Suddenly, Sam woke out of the dream and bolted upright in bed. "My God!" he said. "Of course! Jesse!"

TWENTY-FIVE

During the flight home, Alice noticed that Sam was becoming more and more distant. She, too, felt a growing sense of unease. At one point, she placed her hand on Sam's, saying, "Are we okay?"

"I'm not sure," he said.

"I'm sure about one thing," Alice replied, as Sam looked into her eyes.

"And what's that?"

"I'm sure of who we are. And I'm sure we'll do the right things."

Sam smiled gently and squeezed her hand. Then he laid his head back, closed his eyes, and once again, went back over the event fifteen years ago that had destroyed his son's life.

He had come home early that evening. Alice and Carol had taken Christopher and Jennifer to friends' houses for sleepovers, then he and the two women had taken four-year-old Jesse out for hamburgers. They'd returned home at 7:30, and Jesse had gone into his room to change into his pajamas. Carol and Alice began talking and Sam went into the study. Before they'd realized it, nearly half an hour had gone by with no sign of the boy.

Then he heard Carol call out to Alice. To this day, Sam vividly recalled the odd tone in her voice, and how, at first, he hadn't given it much thought.

Then came Alice's call to him. The fear and urgency were unmistakable and still resonated in Sam's mind. He ran into Jesse's room and, at first, remembered being puzzled, but also thinking his son was playing some sort of a game.

The boy was sitting naked on the carpeted floor, facing away from him, Alice, and Carol, staring up at the wall beside his bed. On the wallpaper, Sam saw a group of odd-looking crayon scribbles. This seemed strange by itself because he knew they had not been there earlier and it was unlike Jesse to have drawn them. But as Sam stepped forward, he noticed something else. The more he looked at them, the more the scribbles seemed to have a kind of symmetry and order to them. They were a series of seven repetitive oval and rectangular shapes, each about four inches in diameter. Sam remembered thinking that the scribbled lines inside and around them almost looked like primitively drawn hieroglyphics of some sort.

Though Jesse was facing away from him, he could see

that the boy appeared to be mesmerized, looking up at the markings and slowly rocking back and forth. As Sam took a step forward and said the boy's name, Jesse didn't turn around to acknowledge. Instead, he raised his arms into the air and began waving them in slow circular motions. At the same time, he began to roll his head back and to the side. As he did this, Sam remembered hearing a slight whining and moaning sound.

He'd called the boy's name a second time, and when he got no answer he was suddenly gripped by a wave of paralyzing fear. He relived the moment now as if it were yesterday. As much as he loved the boy and felt something was terribly wrong, for an instant he couldn't bring himself to step forward.

In that moment's hesitation, Alice had rushed to Jesse, knelt beside the boy and swung him around, saying, "Jesse!"

A sudden look of horror came over Alice's face. Sam looked down and saw what had caused it. Jesse had changed. His eyes had gone distant and dull and his jaw had dropped open. A slight bit of drool slid from the corner of his mouth. His arms were still waving and Sam could see that his whines and moans were not from pain, but rather an attempt to communicate. He was trying to say something. The alert, intelligent son they had eaten hamburgers with only minutes earlier, had suddenly lost his ability to speak.

Sam rushed forward, grabbed Jesse by his shoulders and shook the boy, shouting, "Jesse! Jesse!" Seeing no change, he swept his son up into his arms, turned to Alice and said, "Call 9-1-1!"

Forty-five minutes later Sam and Alice stood beside a tubular metal bed in the Paseo Oaks Hospital, watching as a doctor went through a series of reflex and communication tests. Next came a brain scan.

The initial diagnosis was catastrophic. Jesse had appeared to have suffered some sort of stroke.

More tests showed that the boy's neuronal activity had changed drastically, but the cause remained a mystery. He was no longer able to speak and he had lost much of his coordination and motor skills, but more scans and x-rays showed no brain damage. After two hours, the doctor had simply said, "I can't find any damage, but he's obviously had some sort of severe regression."

"Is it permanent?" Sam asked.

"I have no idea. I want to bring in a neurosurgeon first thing in the morning who may be able to answer some of our questions."

That had given the family hope, but not for long.

After two days and an extensive series of MRIs, comprehension tests, and physical examinations, the neurosurgeon had no better answer. "I can only tell you this," he said. "Your son's brain appears to be healthy and normal and he's suffered no stroke, loss of tissue, or physical trauma. Nevertheless his brain *functions* are very abnormal. What has caused this, I simply can't say. And as for how long it will last, your guess is as good as mine. Believe me, I'd love to tell you he might come out of it tomorrow or next week, but I'd be guessing."

And so the days and weeks had begun to slip by. One specialist after another came up baffled. Soon the weeks became months, and then years, and the changes everyone hoped for never came. Alice had found escape in alcohol and eventually sought help from a therapist. Sam had withdrawn personally and buried himself in his work. And under a shroud of unrelenting depression and hopelessness, the family was left to go on with their lives wondering what had happened to their beautiful son, and why.

TWENTY-SIX

When Sam and Alice arrived home from Africa, Carol welcomed them, but she quickly sensed the couple's need to remain quiet about what had happened on their journey. After asking several questions to which she received nervous glances and illusive answers, she left the couple alone, assuming that when the time was right they would open up to her.

That afternoon the couple spent time with Jesse. They took him for a long walk along the creek and shared a picnic lunch. As Alice fed her son, continually wiping the crumbs and mayonnaise from his mouth, she remembered the small perfect lips as he had eaten ice cream on the night of his ordeal. She visualized his tiny hands wrapped around the sugar cone, his tongue licking, eyes looking up at her wide with innocence and excitement...

Later they played in Jesse's exercise room and together helped change his clothes and massage his limbs. Sam rubbed the boy's pale, sinewy thighs and managed a smile as Jesse arched his back and neck in delight.

"That feel good, Jesse boy?" he whispered.

Jesse cooed and laughed, drool gathering at the corner of his mouth.

Finally, all three and Carol ate an early dinner and the group snuggled up on the couch to watch Jesse's favorite cartoons.

As these events took place, Jesse sensed something was different. But it was a good thing. On this day, the ones he loved most were closer to him for some reason, and smiling and touching him in a new way. They loved him, and he was important to them, and there was something else...

That evening, Sam and Alice put their son to bed in the Constellation Wing and stood above him for several minutes after he'd fallen asleep. Finally, Sam signaled Alice to step outside. It was a warm, comfortable night and the couple walked together through a light breeze to their backyard gazebo. For several moments, Sam stood quietly, looking out into the darkness. "Tell me what you think about all this," he finally said, taking a seat.

"I'm not sure."

"Not sure about what—the experience or what we should do now?"

Alice thought about this. "When we were there...when we woke up in the jungle, there was no doubt in my mind, no fear. Just enlightenment, that wonderful feeling of spiritual discovery."

"And now?"

"Now I'm... I don't know."

Sam looked up into the brilliant night sky and for a moment remained silent. Finally he turned to Alice. "No one in their right mind will believe it actually happened," he said.

"*Was* it real, Sam? I mean we experienced it, but, God!"

"Yes. It was. That's the incredible part...and the hard part."

"Why?"

"Because a place like that can't exist, Alice. What happened to us was physically impossible. Chris was right. There *was* a reason for it...for *us* to be there."

"Well, that's a good thing, right?"

"Think about what that means to the rest of our lives. Everything we know and do. Our friends, our work, our plans."

Alice moved close and the couple hugged, but said nothing. As the breeze picked up slightly, they remained quiet. A short time later, they went back into the house and soon were in bed.

Alice slept restlessly. At 3:30 a.m., she woke and discovered that Sam was not beside her. She leaped out of bed and found him in the family room seated in the dark in front of an unlit fireplace. She sat beside him. "Are you alright?" she asked.

He continued to stare into the darkness of the fireplace. "I remember those scribbled images on the wall in Jesse's room as if it were yesterday," he said. "I remember my son's ruined face and mind, and I remember crying and wondering what in God's name could possibly have happened to him. I remember ripping off the shreds of wallpaper, thinking why us? Why our son? I remember all the years of you crying, and...and now this? How can a place like that exist? Why did we experience it? And what does it mean for Jesse?" He turned to Alice. "The answers to all those questions are in Africa."

TWENTY-SEVEN

Early the next morning, Sam stepped into his study and closed the door. He sat, thought through what he was about to say, then called his executive vice president, Tom Marsh.

Marsh answered jovially, "Hi Sam! Hey, buddy, how was the trip?"

"You wouldn't believe me if I told you, Tom."

"Oh-oh. That doesn't sound so great. Chris okay?"

"He's fine. We met with him, and he's doing great."

"Wonderful!"

Following this came an awkward pause. Sam broke the silence. "I've got a question for you, Tom."

"Shoot."

"It's a big question and an important one. I want you to think about it before you give me your answer."

Marsh remained silent.

"Could you run Waltrick if I put it in your hands? And would you want to?"

"Run it? You mean president?"

"Right."

Again, there was a moment of silence. Finally Marsh said, "Are you serious, Sam?"

"Yes."

"What the hell's going on?"

"First, answer the question."

"Of course I can run it. And hell yes, I'd want to. I'd love to. You know that. But what's this all about?"

"It's about me and Alice going back to Africa for an extended stay."

"What the hell happened over there, Sam?"

"Like I said, Tom, you'd never believe me. Let me just say the trip changed things."

"Sam I think you'd better—"

"Tom, listen to me. The decision is made on my end. If you're sure this is what you want, I'm going to make a very quick announcement to retire."

"Sam, you need to think about this. Waltrick is your life, buddy, your *baby*. Christ, you built it! Give it some time to—"

"I don't need time. I know now what I need to do. How about you?"

"If you're absolutely sure."

"I am."

"Then, hell, I'm ready."

"Good. Set up a meeting with the senior staff for tomorrow morning."

"Done."

TWENTY-EIGHT

When the couple sat down with Carol, Alice began. "I'm sorry we were so distant yesterday," she said.

"I understand," Carol said, "but is everything okay?"

"Yes. Okay, but different. Things are going to be very different now."

Carol held her breath.

"We met Christopher in Africa," Alice continued, "and, well, he'd been right. He'd found something amazing...life changing."

Carol said nothing.

"We found it, too," Sam added.

"What?" Carol asked.

"A spiritual awakening," Alice said.

Carol sat, staring dumbfounded at both Sam and Alice.

"We have to go back, Carol," Alice continued. "And we have to take Jesse."

Carol immediately stood up. "But Alice, you can't—"

"Carol," Sam interrupted, "please listen and please trust us. We need that right now."

Carol slowly took her seat.

"Alice and I talked about whether we should tell you what happened over there, and it's so...bizarre, that at first it seemed the best thing was just keep it a secret from you and everyone else."

"But you're part of our family," Alice added, "and we decided we couldn't do that. We want to tell you the whole story and we want you to come back with us. We want you to help us with Jesse and share this just like we've shared our entire lives."

We want you to come back with us...help us with Jesse... we've shared our entire lives... The words resonated in Carol's mind. Things were about to change. Something had happened—something strange and huge and frightening. But whatever it was, she would be a part of it. They wanted and needed her. Jesse needed her.

TWENTY-NINE

Jennifer was about to leave her office when the phone rang. She looked up at the clock: 6:35 p.m. She was beat. She considered walking out and letting the caller leave a voice mail, but her work ethic won out. "Shit," she said throwing her purse and coat across her desk and moving to the phone.

The voice was calm. "Hi, Jenn. It's Dad."

"Hi, Dad."

"How are things?"

"Fine. What's up? Where are you guys?"

He hesitated slightly. "We're just back from Africa."

Maybe she had been wrong, Jennifer thought. Maybe everything was okay. Maybe they had discovered Christopher's con and were done with it. "Great. Everything okay with Chris?"

"Yes." Again the hesitation. "Actually, things are...well they're fine, honey."

"Is something wrong, Dad?"

"Yes and no. Jenny, can you come down and visit for a night? Your mother and I have something important to talk with you about."

Jennifer tensed. She'd been right. And from the tone of the words she'd just heard, it was probably worse than she'd first thought. "Listen, Dad, whatever it is, you're not going to leave me hanging on a phone call. Yes. I'll come down, but tell me now what's wrong."

Sam hesitated again.

"Dad, for God's sake, what is it? Is something wrong with Mom or Chris?"

"Honey, no. Nothing's wrong with them. We're all fine. And I mean that."

"Jesse?" Jennifer asked.

"Jesse's fine, too."

"Then what the hell's going on?"

"Your Mom and I are going to take Jesse back with us to Africa."

For an instant this threw Jennifer, because it almost sounded like her father was talking about a vacation or some sort of trip. But suddenly she put together the tone in his voice and the message. "What? For a trip or something?"

"No."

"What then?"

"Honey, it's so hard to explain on the phone. I—"

"Dad, tell me, damn it!"

"Your mother, Chris, Jesse, and I may be staying in Africa for a while. We've found something... I can't explain. That's the hard part. We found a very special place and there's a mystery about it—something spiritual that we haven't been able to figure out. We think Jesse can help. And it might help him."

"Jesse? How in the world could Jesse possibly—?" Suddenly a terrible fear began to rise in Jennifer's mind. Chris! Had he actually *succeeded* in getting them swept up in his scam? Could that possibly have happened? With her Dad? Sam Waltrick? "Is this still about Chris and his latest scam?"

Again there was a long pause. Finally her dad said the words that she dreaded. "It's not a scam, honey. I know it's hard to believe, but—"

"But what?"

"But it's true. What Chris has found over there is incredible. Honey, it's a source of spiritual enlightenment."

"Dad, my God! You can't be serious! What's he done to you? Brainwashed you both? Dad, this is *Christopher*, your son. Remember?"

"Honey, of course I remember, but this is different. It's real."

"What? What's real?"

"A place."

"What place?"

"A place where there's a kind of...awakening."

Jennifer couldn't believe what she was hearing. What in the world could Chris have possibly exposed them to in order to bring about this kind of change in her father? It seemed impossible. Suddenly she had a thought. "Dad, what about Mom. Is she there?"

"Yes, she is. You want to speak to her?"

Jennifer could feel her heart pounding. "Yes, put her on."

A moment later her mother's voice came on the line. Again, there was a subtle difference.

"Hi, sweetie."

"Mom, what's going on?"

"Jenny, your dad is right. Chris has found a place in Africa that has some kind of, I don't know, some spiritual quality."

"Mom, have you guys been talking to any religious groups?"

"No, honey. We just—"

"Have you taken anything?"

"What do you mean?"

"I mean like drugs. Have you taken any drugs, drunk, eaten, or smelled anything out of the ordinary?"

"Sweetheart, your father and I are just fine. In fact, we've never been better. I mean that. Nothing's been done to us. We really need to speak with you and tell you what we've found. And how Jesse should be a part of it. And actually, we'd like you to be a part of it, too."

"Mom—"

"Jenn, please. Trust us and come and talk. That's all we ask. Hold your feelings until then... Please?"

Jennifer could tell she wasn't going to change their minds. "Fine," she said. "When should I come?"

"How about Saturday?"

"I'll be there."

"Good. Honey, we love you and please don't worry about us. You'll understand."

As Jennifer hung up the phone, she became more and more upset and angry at her brother. What in God's name had he done this time? On one hand, she couldn't wait to find out. On the other, she dreaded what she might hear.

She thought about her father's words, a source of spiritual enlightenment.

Suddenly she remembered the article she had scanned on the Internet about the spores that caused hallucinations. She drove straight home and went back to that Internet site. She printed out the article and read it over carefully.

THIRTY

The next morning, when Sam Waltrick stepped into a hastily called executive meeting, he was not the same man most of the eighteen executives in attendance had known for many years. The differences quickly became apparent as he stepped through the conference room doors.

He entered with less force and dominance than the tough, determined chief executive who only a few days ago had commanded the head chair at this long mahogany table. Rather than looking like an assault—Sam's usual mode of entrance—he walked in slowly, almost floating through the large, frosted glass doors toward the waiting group. Also missing was the signature Waltrick glare. Replacing it was an oddly contemplative glance around the room at the various faces. Amazingly, the CEO's face even seemed to carry a slight smile.

The most apparent change, however, was in Sam's words—the way he began to speak calmly, quietly, and actually empathizing as he sat down. He looked up at the group of vice presidents and directors and said, "Good morning. I know how busy you all are and I realize this meeting was called very quickly, so I appreciate you being here."

All eighteen faces stared at him, each one trying to read the CEO's thoughts, knowing something big was about to be announced. A trip to Africa. Rumors of a family crisis and a son stranded in Nairobi. And now this—a meeting called on a moment's notice by a strangely passive and empathetic Sam Waltrick.

"I know you're probably all wondering what's been going on with me and my family. And frankly, my plan was to not even bring it up at this meeting, but since I've worked so closely with you all for many years, and you've helped me build the company that up until a few days ago was the central focus of my life, I feel I have to be straight with you."

"*...up until a few days ago.*" Yes! They'd all heard it. This *was* big.

"I've decided to retire immediately," Sam continued, placing a hand on the shoulder of Tom Marsh, who was seated immediately to his right. "And Tom, here, will take over as president and CEO."

After a wave of whispers and gasps, the room became dead quiet.

"And without getting into too much detail, I want to tell you why. I think you all know I was called to Africa by my son, Chris. Most of you know we haven't been on the best of terms for the past few years. Nonetheless, he called my wife and me, and we went. He said he wanted to share something amazing with us. Something...spiritual. I assumed Alice and I would have to deal with more of his irresponsibility, but we found something else."

He hesitated for a moment. The group was mesmerized. Most could not believe what they were hearing, including Tom Marsh. Sam Waltrick and the word "spiritual" simply didn't exist in the same universe.

"We found answers. And some very important questions. I could never begin to explain these to you, so I won't try. But the point is I have to go back. My family and I are leaving immediately for what may be an extended stay in Africa."

The group was stunned. Had Sam Waltrick actually gone off the deep end? Could he have been conned or brainwashed somehow? His words alone were enough to leave everyone in the room in shock, but what happened next floored them.

Sam stood up, his eyes becoming glassy. "Forgive me for being emotional. It's been a very emotional experience for me. I'm going to stop and let you get back to your work now."

Many in the room sat perfectly still holding their breath, trying not to show the extent of their discomfort. The experience was now bordering on becoming downright bizarre. It seemed their leader had changed personalities virtually overnight. The invincible Sam Waltrick was on the fast track to the funny farm and he was heading off into the sunset right before their eyes.

Sam looked around the room. "I know what you're all thinking. I hope one day, you're as lucky as I am. Goodbye."

He turned and walked away from the table.

No one said a word.

He opened the conference room doors, stepped out, and disappeared.

One vice president turned to a colleague and whispered, "Holy fucking Christ!"

THIRTY-ONE

At least, Mitchell Solomon thought, Sam had made good on his word. After an awkward meeting in the Human Resources Department, during which the HR Director, with Solomon's boss as a witness, had taken him step by step through his 'rights of termination,' he'd signed release papers and returned to his office with a check for $195,000. Comfortable indeed!

His first thought was to do exactly as Mason had suggested—get his hands on a hot "escort" and forget his troubles. As he was contemplating this idea, Dana, the pool secretary, stepped into his office. Head cocked and looking appropriately sad, she held out her arms. They shared a ceremonial hug and she passed on the standard ego booster line about one door opening as another one closes. Solomon thanked her. As she was turning to leave, she stopped. "By the way," she said, "did you hear about Sam's little whirlwind trip to Africa?"

"Yeah. Did you hear why?"

"No clue. Leslie said he just dropped everything."

"They're all in a big staff meeting right now."

"Something's up."

Solomon thought about the call Sam had received when they were in his office. He knew the CEO had a flaky son who'd left home and a mentally disabled boy. And he'd heard that Sam's wife was a recovering alcoholic.

"Probably his wife," Dana said. "I've heard the family's all screwed up."

"Did you hear where in Africa?"

"Not a clue. But I did hear he's acting weird now. Anyway, I'm really going to miss you, Mitch. We all are. We just can't understand why he didn't let stinky old McCannon or Damoni go instead of you."

Solomon smiled and thanked her again. When she left he looked around the office. Time to pack. He needed boxes. He started down to the shipping room to see what he could find, but when he stepped into the elevator, without rationalizing, he pushed for the lobby instead.

Twenty minutes later, he found himself stepping into a local synagogue. He had no idea why. He was hardly a religious man, and he didn't feel any need for a spiritual boost. If fact, the waves of panic were giving way more and more to a sense of release and positive anticipation. But now, staring at the brightly lit Ark and Star of David, for some inexplicable reason he felt he was exactly where he needed to be.

THIRTY-TWO

In much the same way Sam's executives recognized that something had changed in their leader, Jane Dawson recognized similar changes in Alice Waltrick. After years of weekly sessions, Jane knew Alice like the back of her hand. The woman, who had first come to her in the throws of deep depression and battling an alcohol addiction, had evolved over time into what Jane considered a functionally impaired woman. Though Alice was not, and probably would never again, be the happy, optimistic woman she once was, she had become capable of understanding what had changed in her, and of adapting to, and living with, that reality.

Knowing very well this back-story about her patient, when Alice stepped into the small, plush office and took her usual seat in the overstuffed plaid chair, several visual signals registered for Jane immediately. Most evident was her patient's body language and the lack of tremors. Alice's norm was to start her sessions sitting perfectly straight with her hands together, fingers touching, resting on her lap.

This was a protective posture, Jane knew, that allowed Alice to feel composed, normal, and experience minimal tremors. Today, however, Alice took her seat and rested her arms out away from her body, on the raised arms of the chair.

Jane immediately glanced at her hands. No shaking.

The next thing that occurred to Jane was how Alice made eye contact so quickly and easily. In the early years, when the trauma of her son's debilitating regression had gripped her like a nightmare, and the shame of her alcohol addiction had eroded her self-esteem, she rarely made eye contact at all. Over time, and after two stays is rehab, she'd gained control over her addiction. She was able to look Jane squarely in the face at that point, but even up until their last session, an awkwardness and discomfort remained visible deep in her large brown eyes.

Today, amazingly, that awkwardness and discomfort were absent. This would seem to have been cause for celebration, and for a few moments Jane almost smiled, wondering just what in the world had happened on this impromptu, out of town trip that had sat so well with Alice. But in the next few moments, Jane thought she saw something different. It wasn't the usual, not the ominous residue of years of sadness and pain because of what had happened to first her youngest, and then her oldest son.

It was something new. A kind of dazed, false calm. It was not the Alice she knew so well, whose psychological scar tissue had hardened over the years from raw mental anguish and times of near insanity, into a survival mode of focused control, frequent nausea, and tremors. It was an Alice who sat before her strangely calm on the eve of a great storm. It was an Alice who had somehow shoved aside all the protective barriers and faced something big, and now felt that she could stand with perfect balance at the edge of the precipice. It was an Alice, Jane was suddenly convinced, in great psychological danger.

"Hi, kid," Jane said.

Alice knew that Jane was acting casual, but watching her intently, wondering, knowing something was different. "Hi, Jane," she replied.

"So, a trip, huh? Was it a good one?"

"Yes."

"And you actually got that workaholic husband of yours to take you?"

"He didn't want to at first, but he came through."

"I can't believe that. That is so great!"

"We saw Christopher, Jane."

Of course! Jane thought. That was it. Christopher! He'd been physically absent from her life for three years and she'd pined every day for him. Seeing him could have been a wonderful, cathartic experience. Or... "Goodness. How exciting! How is he?"

"He's well. Great, in fact."

"And he and Sam?"

"Believe it or not, they're okay now."

"Wow! This must have been some trip! I'm delighted for you, Alice. This is something you've wanted for years."

"Yes."

After a long pause, Jane knew there was more to the story, and she felt it was not going to be positive. "So is he coming home?"

"Actually no, he's staying."

"Oh? Where?"

"Africa."

"Africa! You went to Africa?"

Alice nodded and smiled.

"Well, for goodness sake. Tell me about it! What's in Africa?"

Alice hesitated and gathered her thoughts. Jane knew the truth was about to come out. She felt a long forgotten, but now familiar, tension rising in her gut just as it had years ago in her early sessions with Alice, the woman who had become her long-time friend...the person she had protected. The one...

"Jane, I'm leaving for a while. Maybe for a long time. Sam's retiring and we're both going to Africa to be with Chris."

Jane sat speechless.

"I'm not sure when...or if we'll be back. You and I have been so close over the years, and you've done so much for me...been there and listened...and helped me finally get clarity and control. I know I wouldn't be sitting here today if it wasn't for you."

Jane had gone pale. Alice could see the shock on her face as she started to speak. "Are you, I mean, is this...are you sure it's—"

"Yes. It's the right thing. Sam and I have been over it and we've weighed everything very carefully."

"But, hon, it's so fast! God, *what happened?*"

"It's very hard to explain. Sam and I found something... a place we've been searching for and both needed."

The tears began to well up in Alice's eyes. Jane felt an inexplicable surge of emotion suddenly surface in her as well. It was unprofessional, she knew, and totally unlike her, but she left her chair, moved to Alice, and knelt, taking her longtime friend's hands in her own. "Alice, honey, I don't think—"

Alice leaned forward.

"Yes. It is. It really is the right thing. I can't tell you why, Jane. You have no idea how much I want to, but I can't. I can only tell you that I'll be okay from now on. You don't have to worry. Where I'm going and what we've found, I'm fine now. And so is Sam, and Christopher and hopefully Jennifer."

"Alice, for God's sake, just stop for minute!"

Alice got to her feet, crying openly.

Jane stood up.

"I love you," Alice said, and hugged Jane.

Jane held her friend, an uncontrollable wave of emotion welling up.

Alice broke away and turned toward the door.

"Alice, my God!"

Just as Alice stepped through the door, she looked back over her shoulder and saw her therapist and friend of so many years, eyes squinted with emotion, holding her hands up to her mouth. She saw Jane's chest heave once. She saw deep sadness and bewilderment. Alice closed the door, hurrying through the waiting room to the exit.

THIRTY-THREE

Three nights after their telephone conversation, Jennifer stepped into her parents' house. After the usual hugs and kisses, the group sat in the kitchen. Jennifer got straight to the point. "So tell me what happened to you two," she said.

"What happened," Sam said, "is something amazing."

As her father said this, Jennifer immediately looked toward her mother for a reaction. Alice sat calmly beside her husband with a gentle smile on her face. She obviously took no argument with what Sam was about to say.

"Amazing, like how?" Jennifer asked.

Sam paused. Jennifer could tell he was searching for the right words. Finally, her father spoke. "Jennifer, before I tell you about this, I want you to remember the type of people your mother and I are. We're not prone to being impulsive, and we're certainly not the type to be taken in by some con or harebrained scheme."

"I know you're not."

"When we got Chris's call to meet him in Africa, that's exactly what your dad and I thought was in store for us," Alice said.

"I was absolutely positive he'd stumbled into another one of his 'change the world' scams or New Age dropout groups."

"And we were going to have to go bail him out again," Alice added.

Jennifer watched them both as they spoke. They seemed fine. It was nearly the parents she knew now speaking to her—level headed, direct, sincere. But there was one subtle change she sensed in them—a kind of calm or passive tone that was uncharacteristic of her father.

"But that wasn't the case I take it? You didn't have to bail him out?"

"No," Sam said.

"So what did you find?"

Again Sam hesitated, glancing over at Alice. "We found an amazing place," she said. "A place in the jungle where—"

"Where there's a very deep insight into our world," Sam said.

They hesitated again. "I don't get it, Dad," Jennifer said. "What kind of insight? You keep talking about this place, but you're not being specific. What did you have to do to get this insight? Did you take anything?"

Both Sam and Alice knew in their hearts Jennifer wouldn't be persuaded. The simple truth was, she was very much like her father, opinionated and forceful. To convince her of what they had experienced would be virtually impossible without her actually experiencing it herself. Before she'd come this evening they'd both hoped in their hearts they would be able to get through to her. But now that she was seated in front of them, their feelings were changing.

"The only thing they gave us was something to make us sleep on our way to the place," Alice said. The look on Jennifer's face told them that they had just confirmed her suspicions. They were right.

They had taken something, she thought to herself. Of course they had. What else, other than something like the Spider Eye spores, could explain this erratic behavior? But she remained quiet in this thought because she wanted to know more—more about what that bastard of a brother had gotten them into this time.

"It wasn't any kind of mind altering drug," Alice added. "We woke up from it feeling perfectly normal."

"Then why take it?"

"Because they took us to a secret place."

"What kind of place?"

"A place in the jungle. A path that led to a kind of natural bridge."

"And were there other people there?"

"No. Just your mother and me."

Again Sam paused and looked at his wife. Jennifer decided to press for specifics. "Okay, so what happened then?"

Sam took a deep breath. "We crossed," he said, "and that's when a change took place."

"What kind of change?"

Both Sam and Alice hesitated. Finally Sam spoke. "We changed both physically and mentally… We became, we reverted to…a kind of primitive form."

Jennifer suddenly felt clammy and as if she were about to hyperventilate. Though she tried to hide it, she knew her parents could see her becoming pale and horrified before their eyes. After an awkward moment of silence she took a deep breath, lifted the Internet article out of her purse, and placed it on the table.

"Mom and Dad," she said, her voice quavering, "please listen to me and please keep an open mind. Will you do that for me? Please?"

The couple nodded. "Yes," they said in unison.

"This is an article I came across on the 'net. It was written by a professor, actually a doctor with very impressive credentials. It's about a plant called the Spider Eye that grows only in certain places in Africa, places near where you were. And it gives off spores of some kind that are hallucinogenic. The article says that for centuries it helped sustain a cult called the "Sacred Journey." Members who were exposed to the spores thought they'd been part of God-like experiences. They'd come from all over Africa on these journeys, and they'd have spiritual 'awakenings.' But it was all in their heads. And these days the spores are being studied for medical uses, but they've also been used to con people—mostly Europeans and Americans.

"Now think about it, Dad. Just step back for a second and think logically. That's all I'm asking. Doesn't it make sense that if this drink you took didn't cause some kind of delirium, it could have been used to just get you to a place where spores like this might do it? Isn't there at least a *possibility* that could have happened?"

Sam picked up the article and looked at it. Alice stepped

up to his side. Could it have been possible, both were thinking at the same moment? A sinking feeling settled in their stomachs.

Sam sat down and scanned the article. Alice stood at his side, also reading. After several minutes Sam spoke. "Your logic follows," he said finally to his daughter. "It definitely could have been something like this…and Jennifer, sweetheart, I love you for finding this and bringing it here to us. And I love you for having the guts to do what you're doing right now. But, honey, it wasn't this."

Jennifer's heart sank.

"What we experienced was not a hallucination. It was real. It was as real as you standing in front of me right now. We could smell it, touch it, feel it. We were perfectly clear headed, and it was the same for both of us."

"Do you hear what you're telling me?" Jennifer pleaded. "Listen to yourselves. Dad, you're the founder and CEO of a major law firm! And Mom, you're educated and intelligent! Christ, you were a teacher! How can you both sit here and tell me you went to sleep, woke up in some jungle, and crossed a bridge that changed you into another life form? My God! Don't you get it? You've been tricked! You've been made to believe another one of that little son-of-a-bitch's—"

"Stop it!" Sam snapped, suddenly throwing the article across the room. "Is that what you think of us? That we're weak minded and gullible? That some drug, or even worse, some scam could change our whole lives? That we could be taken in by that kind of thing? Is that the kind of respect you have for us?"

Jennifer felt her temples throbbing. She struggled to maintain her composure.

"Did it ever occur to you that we *might* just be intelligent enough to recognize a scam?"

Jennifer fought to regain her composure. With great effort, she got her emotions under control. "Okay. Okay. I'm sorry. Tell me everything about this…change."

Alice looked at Sam. After a moment's hesitation, she said, "She'll never believe us, Sam."

Sam knew his wife was right. This had been a mistake.

"Please," Jennifer said.

After a long pause, Sam began. "We changed in a good way."

"In a way that opened our eyes," Alice added.

"How so?"

"We've realized that as human beings, we've lost something very valuable."

They could see that with every word they said Jennifer was becoming more convinced they had gone over the deep end.

"You mean you two? Or all of us—humanity?"

"Humanity," Sam said.

Jennifer got to her feet and wheeled around. "Oh, Christ. Here it comes, right? You discovered some…some new universe or some crazy communal way of life. That son of yours has gone and twisted both your heads into believing the world is going to end or some goddamned thing, so you're going to go live in the bush or something. Right?"

Sam and Alice both remained quiet after this outburst.

"Don't you two see? Think about it! *Please, think!* He

talks you into going to some place in the middle of nowhere, gives you some sleeping potion, and you wake up thinking your lives have been a waste! It fits the pattern! It's him, Dad. Chris! He's somehow managed to pull off the biggest con of his life. He's gotten you two sucked into some damned cult or scam and you don't even know it! You can't even see it! You two are—"

Sam stood up. "*Damn it, stop!*" he yelled and slammed his palm down onto the table. Alice flinched and began to cry. Sam continued in what Jennifer could see was a state of controlled rage. "Your mother and I have found a place that holds the truth about our existence. Some of that truth we've already discovered. We feel that Jesse will provide the final pieces of the puzzle. We're taking him back to Africa on Monday, and we would like you to come, too."

Jennifer stood, unable to speak, staring at her mother and father.

THIRTY-FOUR

Shortly after her father's outburst, Jennifer said she could not spend the night. Sam and Alice pleaded with her to at least give them the benefit of the doubt, to come and witness what they were talking about. And though she said she would give it some thought, she would not commit. Instead, she insisted that she had to spend some time alone. As she was leaving, Sam apologized and told her he would hold a place for her on the charter flight he had arranged. If she didn't come, he said, her seat would remain open.

Then she was gone.

Jennifer went straight to a hotel and called Aaron. "I didn't want to get you involved in this," she said. "I don't want you to think my family is screwy, but I need to talk."

"I'm glad you called," Aaron said. "What's up?"

After explaining what her parents had told her, he agreed Sam and Alice had somehow been unknowingly drugged and perhaps hypnotized or brainwashed by a cult of some kind. Jennifer asked if Aaron knew any way she could stop them from taking Jesse and returning to Africa.

"The problem is," Aaron said, "they're wealthy, respected people and Jesse is their son. And he's not a minor. They can basically do anything they want with him. Unless—"

"Unless what?"

"Unless you can somehow prove they've gone over the hill, and because Jesse is disabled, even though he's legally an adult, he's in danger of being abused."

"Prove it to who? The police?"

"Actually, the courts, I think. I doubt the police can stop them without a court order of some kind."

"That could take forever," Jennifer said.

After a moment, Aaron had an idea. "There may be another way. There's got to be a human services group down there. Maybe part of the city government. I'm not sure, but I think their job is to intervene, or at least check out things like child abuse. And I think they'll act if they get some sort of tip that abuse is going on. They may even have people that deal specifically with the abuse of disabled adults. They might be able to at least stop your folks from taking Jesse out of his home until the courts have a look at it."

Hope sprang up in Jennifer's mind. "You think I can reach them on a weekend?"

"They should have emergency numbers," Aaron said. "Check in the phone book and try first thing in the morning."

"Thanks. I owe you."

"No you don't. Call if I can help some more. In fact, call and let me know what happens either way."

This guy, Jennifer decided, was a keeper. Determined that she would somehow stop this charade and save her family, she went to bed and slept fitfully.

THIRTY-FIVE

The next morning, after several dead-end calls, Jennifer reached a group called Absolve. She found herself talking to a man named Don Haskell. He answered with a flat, uninterested voice, "Absolve, Haskell."

"Hi," Jennifer said. "I have a problem I'd like to get some advice on. Is there someone there I can talk to?"

"What type of problem?"

"Maybe a form of abuse. Abuse of a mentally disabled adult."

"Can you tell me about it?"

"Two family members of mine, actually my mother and my father, have become involved with, I'm not sure what, but they're suddenly on this—I'm afraid they may have joined a cult."

"What makes you say that?"

"They just got back from Africa. That's where all this took place. They went to meet my brother, who's a complete bastard and who's always into some scam. My dad is the

CEO of a large company. He's acting totally out of character and they're going back to Africa on Monday and taking my mentally disabled brother. He has no business being on a plane to Africa!"

"How old is he, ma'am?"

"He's nineteen, but with the IQ of about a two-year-old."

Haskell told Jennifer he could offer no help. His group, he said, worked with the state on interventions involving small children, and they had never gotten involved in an adult case, let alone one involving another country. He said the best he could do was give her the telephone number of a woman he thought had coordinated international rescues from such groups.

Jennifer thanked him, hung up, and immediately called the number. She reached Karen Morris. Unlike Haskell, this woman seemed friendly, compassionate, and concerned. After hearing Jennifer's story, she asked, "I assume your parents have full legal custody of your brother?"

"Yes."

"So that means he's in a private institution? Not on some state- or federally-funded program?"

"No. My parents are very wealthy. They have a full-time nurse, actually, a longtime friend that's lived with us for years. There are also several employees and a wing of our house designed especially for him. And..." Jennifer found herself starting to tear up as she continued. "And he's just never gone very far! He's always been sheltered and kept in a very controlled environment. I mean, God knows how he'll feel, or what he'll think!"

"Are they taking him on a public flight?"

"No. My dad has chartered a plane."

Morris was silent for several moments. "And you feel their actions are motivated by a religious group of some sort?" she asked finally.

"Yes, I'm positive."

"Why is that?"

"The whole thing sounds totally weird. Something about transforming in the middle of the jungle. A special place, a bridge or something, and a small group of people. Everyone changes there, I think they said. My little brother became mentally ill years ago, and since then our family's never been right. I don't know, maybe they think they can cure him. And I read an article about some hallucinogenic spores in the area."

"Did your parents talk at all about money? For instance, have they been asked to finance any of this group's activities or needs? Or maybe loan them money?"

Jennifer thought about this. There had been no talk of money. But it made perfect sense. If Christopher had let it be known how wealthy her parents were, they'd be a perfect target for a scam. She told this to Morris and then poured out everything else she could think of. Finally she said, "The one thing I just can't understand is how they got to my dad. My mother, okay, she's an intelligent woman, but she's also emotional and maybe gullible, especially when it comes to my irresponsible brother. But my dad is a rock. He's a CEO. He's built a huge law business barehanded, and he's tough as nails. I just can't imagine them conning him!" After a long pause Jennifer prodded, "So what can I do?"

"You can file a complaint," Morris said, "and I'll be happy to initiate an investigation."

Hope sprang up in Jennifer, tempered by the anxiety of wondering whether she had just done the right thing.

"But you have to understand," Morris continued, "we can't just run out and invade a family's right to privacy based on a single call. There are guidelines—a face-to-face interview, an affidavit, legal issues. It'll take a few days at least."

"Days! But they're leaving tomorrow morning!"

"Look, if you can tell me that this boy's life is in danger or that he's being physically brutalized or sexually molested, I'll have the police out at your parents' house within the hour. But, before I do that, you need to know these are very serious charges and if they're not substantiated... Can you tell me your brother is in that kind of situation?"

"No."

"Then I'm sorry."

Jennifer hung up feeling hopeless. Should she just call the local police? Suddenly, she thought of Carol. Had her mother and father told her? Convinced her? Jennifer decided she had to find out. She called and immediately discovered that her parents had already gotten to her.

"Jennifer," Carol said, in what sounded like an anxious, or worried tone, "I can understand your reservations, hon, honestly, but—"

"You don't have any reservations?"

"Yes, I do. Frankly, I have some serious reservations, but the bottom line is I trust your mother and father. I have to. I know how much they both love your brother and I know that whatever is behind this has become so important to them they feel they have to follow through with it. I can't stand in the way of that, honey. I have to help and support them. They've done so much for me, especially your mom."

"Fine," Jennifer responded. "Everyone's supporting everyone. But how about Jesse? Isn't anyone concerned about him! Think about how he'll feel, how confused and scared he might be!"

"I'm going along. I'll be with your brother every minute, and sweetie, I'm not involved in this religious thing at all."

"You're going, too?"

"Absolutely."

"And how about when you get to Africa?"

"Your dad is making arrangements. Everything. Jenn, it's going to be okay. I wouldn't let your brother get hurt for anyone. Believe me, I won't leave his side."

It seemed Jennifer had no way to stop this horrible mistake from happening. It was then that, what at first seemed like a crazy idea, began to take shape in her mind. Suppose she took her dad up on the offer and went along to see what this was all about. It was a bizarre and frightening thought. She would have to leave work virtually without notice. She could pull that off, but she had no idea what she would be getting herself into. But maybe she could make contact with the local police. Maybe they could stop it. Or, if there was no other way, maybe she could stop it herself. It was a long shot, but there seemed to be no choice. After hanging up on Carol and vacillating for nearly an hour, she made her decision.

She called her parents, and in a frank tone said she still did not believe them, but she had decided to do as her father had asked, and trust them. She would withhold judgment, she said, and come along on the trip. In truth, the only thing she intended to find out was what type of scam this was and how she could rescue her family from it.

THIRTY-SIX

Jesse knew something different was happening even before the large limo-van arrived. In his world of sounds, images, and colors, very slight changes told him this. As those he loved had first come together surrounding him, he experienced the feelings in his mind and his stomach that signaled their love and caring. When they had arrived, the motions of their bodies and their voices caused the feelings inside him to intensify. This felt right and good. The way his face tightened into an odd, drooling smile and his neck stretched and curved around was an acceptance and thankfulness for their love. The touch of their hands and mouths, the warmth and texture of their skin against his, and the varying sounds of their voices all told Jesse that, although something was different, things were good and his world was intact.

Then, one moved away slightly. The others turned their attention away from Jesse and they made sounds and motions amongst themselves. It was then that their words and the way they faced each other began to signal a more pronounced difference. At first, the change was good and Jesse gave it no thought. But then it seemed to continue and strengthen, to last longer than these things normally did. And there was something about the pace of their movements, the sounds they made, and how the focus of their attention kept changing, flowing back and forth—how it would come to him and hover, then drift away. Finally it showered him, bathed him in their love. In Jesse's mind, all this was not something to become frightened about. It was simply something new and good. And because of this, he felt the feelings in his body speed up again.

Later, they were gone and he found himself alone under the stars of a cloudless night. The brilliant points hung over him like a great, dazzling net. And as they twinkled above him, he thought he could feel the slightest sparkling in his skin. Just as on so many other nights, their sharp brilliance brought him a sense of openness and a kind of thrill he could not experience during the day. As he lay beneath the Milky Way, he almost felt he knew something about it...something about things far away. He had no words to articulate these feelings, but the sense of some vast expanse was with him. As the night sky blazed, the sparkling in his skin confirmed the goodness of this wonderful open feeling. The stars had always been his greatest escape—his gateway to some other place, some other way of knowing the world around him. Far away among them was some grand mystery that he sometimes felt he was actually close to understanding.

These feelings transported Jesse to the part of the cycle

when everything somehow drained out of him and he forgot all things. This was the place where fragments of images would pass through his mind and he would drift through odd places with strange people and events, and some unknown time later he would open his eyes. The stars would be gone and he would realize that his world had once again changed into sunlight.

And this time, just as he sensed the night pass into day, there were still more new changes to experience. More people surrounding him. Soon he was in motion, in a new way. The coolness of the Constellation Wing passed into the warmth and glare of sunlight and bright, windy air. Those who loved him were close by as he was enclosed and again moving, being jostled and held. Following this came new noises and smells, new faces, new rhythms. As he slowly made his way through these changes, they sometimes frightened him, but never enough to become panicky, because those who loved him were near and they shared the experience. They were at his side calming him in the deafening rush of freeway traffic and they guided him through noisy crowds in starkly lit airport hallways. And later they brought him into a new kind of enclosure. It began to move and his stomach rose in his body creating a brand new sensation. They were with him and it was sometimes frightening, sometimes odd, and sometimes wonderful as the aircraft made its way south and east to Africa.

THIRTY-SEVEN

Twenty-three hours later the family group stepped into the African home Sam had rented for this trip. It was a large, ranch-style house in the Nairobi countryside that had recently belonged to an aging government official. Because the official had had severe medical problems the last few years of his life, the house had been converted to include a wing similar to Jesse's in the Waltrick's home. Searched out and secured by Sam's real estate contacts, it served as a perfect temporary quarters.

The group had settled in after a very long flight. Jesse was with Carol getting used to his new quarters and Jennifer, Sam, and Alice had stepped out onto the veranda. The air was fragrant and cool and an expanse of brilliant greens spread before them. Though Jennifer maintained her composure and appeared to be comfortable, she had been churning inside—questioning whether she should have come and horrified by the thought of what might happen.

Then she heard footsteps behind her. Sam and Alice looked up and smiled.

Jennifer turned, and for the first time in three years, saw Christopher.

He smiled, held out his arms, and said, "Hi, Sis."

The instant she saw him she did the last thing in the would she would have thought. She burst into tears, fell into his arms and held him very tightly until the waves of emotion subsided. Then she lifted her head and said quietly, "We have to talk."

Christopher pulled back and gazed into her eyes, still smiling. It was a smile of love. He turned to his parents and said, "Mom and Dad, I need to spend a little time with Jenn. It's been forever."

Sam and Alice got to their feet and went into the house.

Jennifer and Christopher sat down in the long shadows and red sunlight of the waning African day. Jennifer stared into her brother's eyes. She took a deep breath and said, "Chris, first and foremost, please don't insult my intelligence. I want you to tell me what's going on, and remember it's me, your sister. We haven't seen each other in three years, but here's my promise. If I find out you're doing anything to con or harm our parents and Jesse, not only will I not allow it to happen, I will never…never speak to you again. Now please tell me what the hell is going on."

Chris remained smiling. "I understand your promise, Jenn," he said, "and I accept it. In return I can promise you two things. First, I swear to God I will not lie to you. Second, you're not going to believe a word I say."

"Try me."

"There's a place that only a few people on earth know about. It's a very special and a very spiritual place. It's a place where people change, and they gain a new kind of understanding."

Here it comes, Jennifer thought. The con. The bullshit, laid on like none other than her brother could do. "What kind of understanding?"

"About us...the world...God."

"What do you mean when you say people change in this place?"

Christopher knew she wouldn't believe him, so instead he said, "Look, I hope you'll just come with us tomorrow. I've made all the arrangements. You'll see for yourself."

"And do I have to drink something first?"

"Yes."

"Why?"

"Because no one can know where this place is. I don't even know. I have no idea if it's fifty miles or five hundred miles from here. I just know it exists and it's real. And I know if you come and see for yourself, you'll understand."

"If only a few people know where it is, why bring you and Mom and Dad in on it? Why even let them know about it?"

Christopher paused. "Because the woman who found this place is...documenting it. And she believes we can help her."

"Who? You? Mom and Dad?"

"No," Christopher said. "Well, yes *and* no."

"Well, who then?"

Christopher was silent.

Suddenly it became clear to Jennifer. Of course! "Jesse!" she burst out. "Jesse?"

"Yes," Christopher said, "Jesse."

"And you've known this all along?"

"I had a sense."

"And have Mom and Dad known?"

"Not at first, but they do now. Dad figured it out for himself. I swear to you, he's the one who decided to bring Jesse. I never even asked."

"But you knew!"

"Yes, I knew. I mean I *assumed*, but I wasn't sure. Jenn, remember when we were just kids? When Jesse got sick? You and I weren't there that night, and Dad and Mom never really explained, but something strange happened and there's a connection here. Remember those scribbles on the wall?"

As he said this, Christopher took a torn piece of wallpaper from his shirt pocket and handed it to Jennifer. She looked down at the light blue background and patterns of cartoon cowboys. On top of it were several of the scribbled shapes drawn in crayon.

"They're exactly like the ones this woman has in a set of scrolls. And Jesse lost his intelligence that night, his ability to reason and speak. He—"

"And you conned Mom and Dad."

"No, I didn't. I agreed with what they realized. And besides that, it was more than Jesse. I brought them here so *they* could experience this firsthand, too. So they could understand. And they did, Jenn. They did. They discovered exactly what I'd hoped they would." He hesitated. "And I wanted them...and you, too, actually...to come for one other reason. I won't be going home again. I'm going to this place and I've decided to stay."

Jennifer fumed. She had been right. It was all a con. A skillfully choreographed series of events designed to get her little brother into the African jungle for who knew what horrible reason. To "heal" his illness? For a hefty price?

Christopher interrupted the rage he could see building in her. "Jennifer, listen to me. Think whatever you want. Hate me. Believe I'm shit, and decide you'll never speak to me again. Do all of those things, but do me one favor. Just come tomorrow and see. That's all I will ever ask of you. Just come one time and you'll understand. I swear to God you'll understand."

Jennifer turned and walked into the house. She found her mother and father seated together. "He admitted it, Dad! He just admitted it! He's conned you both! It was all designed to get Jesse here!"

Christopher had come in behind her. "Tell them, Christopher. Go ahead!" she yelled.

Christopher faced his father. "I felt there was a connection to Jesse before I called you, at least I *thought* there was. But there was no way I could do anything about it. I knew you'd never bring him, and I didn't even want to suggest it. I had to get you here to experience it. I needed to make you understand for yourselves. And you did. You came and you realized exactly what I knew you would."

Jennifer looked at her parents and waited for a response. What they did and said stunned her.

Alice took her husband's hand and turned to Jennifer.

"It's okay, sweetheart," she said. "Your brother did the right thing."

Jennifer threw up her hands, shook her head, and exclaimed, "Okay, I get it and I give. Jesus Christ, I give! Whatever you've all experienced… There's no question about it. I want to come and see it."

Alice smiled, and so did Sam.

Alice got to her feet, moved to her daughter, and took her in her arms. "You'll see tomorrow, honey," Alice said. "And you'll understand."

THIRTY-EIGHT

That evening the family sat out under the stars of a brilliant African sky.

Jesse sat with them in his wheelchair, his entire mind and body awash in a celestial beauty he had never before experienced. Above him the Milky Way arched across the black sky like a long, silver cloud, skirted by more stars than his eyes had ever seen. He rolled his head and arched his neck in the delight of feelings he had never imagined. Adding to the beauty of the night were the magnificent smells and sounds of the surrounding jungle. They seemed to blend perfectly with the amazing light show overhead forming a great, dark panorama of stunning beauty.

And it was during this experience that something began to grow in Jesse, a feeling of immense breadth and expanse. Like all experiences in his world, he could not have described what he was feeling, but in his own way he was aware of its depth and profundity. He was also aware of those who loved him. Their closeness. Their attunement to his joy. He felt that a kind of meaning was entering him. A new, exciting kind of importance was becoming part of his life.

The rest of the family made small talk, but for most of the evening they were quiet, contemplating the next day's journey and what would follow. Privately, Alice and Sam had mixed feelings. Both sensed they were on the verge of the most important events of their lives, and the spiritual lights that kindled in both of their hearts were dimmed only by the anxiety they felt for their daughter. She had consented to come, but only out of desperation. She did not believe. Would she go through with it? Alice wondered. And, most importantly, *would whatever happened on the next day be for the rest of their lives?*

The Waltricks were at least partly wrong about Jennifer's intent. With the beauty and wildness of the night surrounding her, even Jennifer felt a growing connection to this place. A kind of calmness prodded at the edges of her consciousness like a spark of spiritual realization trying to edge its way into her mind. But, in the end, she would not allow it. Though she acknowledged the feelings, they were not strong enough to make her accept whatever she would experience the next day and shake her commitment to take her parents and brother home to safety.

Christopher suspected that Jennifer might back out, but he did not realize that her concession to the group earlier had simply been a diversion which she hoped would allow her the time to come up with a rescue plan.

THIRTY-NINE

The van arrived shortly after 9:00 a.m.

Everyone in the house was ready, but just before 9:00 Jennifer had gone upstairs saying she would be down in a few minutes. When Alice heard the van pulling up, she looked toward the stairs. Jennifer had come half way down.

"Jennifer?" Alice said, realizing something was wrong.

The group turned.

"I'm sorry," Jennifer said, "I won't be going."

Chris hurried to the base of the stairs. "Jennifer, please," he said.

Jennifer did not answer her brother. She turned to her mother and father. "Mom and Dad, I'm sorry. I know that you're getting into something horrible. Something you'll regret. I wanted to find a way to stop it, but I can't. I'm pleading with you to please not go."

"My God, Sam!" Alice blurted out. "Talk to her!"

"Jenny, honey, we're only asking you to come and *see!* You don't have to do anything. Just come!"

"But I *do* have to do something, Dad, and so do you. Don't you see? You have to drink their drug. You have to lose consciousness. You have no idea what's happening! This place of yours is in your mind. It's a hallucination or a con. It doesn't exist. This is the real world, remember, Dad? You told me. There's no magic. No mysteries. It's all logical!"

"Jenn, no one is going to hurt any of us," Christopher urged. "And it's real, Sis. It's really *real!* You just have to let down that guard for once in your life and experience it!"

Alice burst into tears and ran to her daughter. "Sweetheart, please listen! I can't go and leave you here like this. I can't lose you!"

"But you *are* losing me, Mom. I'm sorry, but you are! Because you've been blinded, and as much as I love you all, I can't go along and watch this happen. I thought I could, but I can't be a part of it."

Carol had been watching Jesse. The boy had begun tensing his entire body and looking from side to side as the voices surrounding him became louder and more emotional. Now Carol saw a demeanor of fear and confusion coming over him. He was straightening his legs, something she'd never seen him do before, and he'd begun rolling his stiffened body to the side. At the same time, a deep moan escaped his lips. His eyes had begun to go wide with fear and uncertainty. Horrified, Carol shouted, "*Please!*" then ran to Jesse's side, knelt, and began trying to calm him. "It's okay sweetheart!" she said, stroking his face and forcing a smile. "It's fine…"

The van honked. Christopher ran outside. As he went

past Sam, he said, "She won't stay. If she thinks there's trouble, she'll go." Then he was out the door.

Sam rushed to his daughter. "Jennifer, haven't you always trusted me?"

"Yes, Dad, I have. You've been the rock in my life. And I love you and Mom both for all you've given me, but *I can't do this!*"

Mother, daughter, and father fell into an embrace, crying in each other's arms.

Jesse let out a sudden howl and rolled his body, nearly toppling out of his wheelchair.

Alice turned to the boy and then looked up at her husband. Sam saw horror in his wife's eyes.

Christopher stepped back into the house. "She's going to leave," he said.

Alice ran to the now convulsive Jesse, tears streaming from her eyes. She hugged and kissed the boy, then turned back to her husband. "Sam," she cried, "go. Hurry and go! I'll stay with Jennifer."

"No!" Carol cried, clutching Jesse's arm. "Please, Sam, *no!*"

Sam's mind raced. "My God, Alice. No!"

"Dad, it's now or never," Christopher said.

"Go," Alice said. "Go and watch over the boys. I'll stay with Jennifer, and we'll be here when you come back. Go!"

"No! I—"

"Jennifer doesn't understand, Sam!" she said, moving back to her daughter's side. "We can't expect her to! And we can't leave her like this—I can't. She's my flesh and blood, for God's sake. Do you think I could possibly leave her alone in this world?"

Sam turned to Jennifer, pleading. "Jenn, honey, God, please!" He held his wife and daughter tightly.

"Dad!" came Christopher's voice.

Sam turned and ran down the stairs. As he reached the bottom Alice screamed out, "Sam!"

He stopped and turned.

"Come back, sweetheart! Go now but, for God's sake, *please come back to me!*"

Jesse had begun to wail and thrash. Holding him tightly, Carol screamed, "No! Sam, No! *You cannot do this!*"

Sam hesitated, and then took the handles of Jesse's wheelchair. Carol screamed, "Jesse! Honey!" hanging on as tightly as she could. After being dragged several feet, she lost her grip and fell to the floor crying hysterically as Sam rushed through the door. He and Christopher lifted Jesse out of the wheelchair and into the van and closed the side door. They pulled away. Alice and Jennifer ran down the stairs and helped Carol to her feet. The three women then rushed out onto the porch, crying as the van drove off.

And two of the women did not know, as they sobbed in each other's arms, that at that moment other eyes were also intently watching the van as it bounced away on the dusty, pothole-ridden dirt road.

FORTY

Several days earlier, when Carol hung up from her phone conversation with Jennifer, her heart had been racing. Though she'd told Jennifer she supported Sam and Alice without question, in truth she'd been terribly worried and suspicious of what might be in store. So suspicious, in fact, that just moments before receiving Jennifer's call, she'd hung up from a call with an old friend of her husband's in the FBI.

Her decision to make the call had come a day earlier, after she'd gone into the Constellation Wing and sat with Jesse as he slept. As she watched him, her thoughts had drifted back to the boy's early years and that bizarre night that had robbed him of his intelligence and personality.

Still struggling with the loss of her husband, Carol had been visiting the Waltricks when the incident occurred. Over the next several months, she'd come and gone several times, sometimes staying for weeks. She remembered helping Alice with the boy as she struggled with her own future as a widow. But she'd also begun to realize that helping poor Jesse gave her something she could no longer find in her own life—a deep sense of purpose and increasing freedom from the paralyzing depression of losing her husband.

Soon six months had passed, then a year. She, Alice, and Sam had slowly come to terms with the knowledge that Jesse would never be normal again, and the only course left was to love him, take care of him, and face whatever the future held with hope, faith, and gratitude that he was still part of their lives.

She recalled the night she'd gone to Sam and Alice and simply said, "I love your son. I love making him happy. And I love both of you. May I stay?" Later that night, she and Alice had sat together in the newly completed Constellation Wing with five-year-old Jesse lying between them under a sparkling, wintry blanket of stars.

Looking down now at the grown but defenseless young man, she wondered how he would take to an airplane flight. He had never been on a plane in his life. And how about Africa, the living conditions? His special requirements? Would he be in danger? Danger to her was one thing. She would face that for the Waltricks without hesitation. But danger to Jesse was something else, something absolutely intolerable to her.

It was then that she had remembered the FBI agent's name—Dale Kilder.

She'd rushed back to her room and found his number.

She made the call and told Kilder everything she knew.

"Definitely sounds strange," he'd said, after hearing the

entire story. "Certainly out of character for two educated and respected people."

"It's bizarre," Carol had answered.

Kilder went on to say he couldn't be sure that anything illegal or dangerous was happening, but he had a contact in Africa he would like to confer with. "In the meantime, can you get some more details for me?" he'd asked.

"What do you need?"

"As much as possible about who these people are they're meeting, and the travel plans—the charter service, arrival time and location, where you're staying, anything like that."

Carol had said she would get whatever information she could. She and Kilder had agreed to talk again the next day, and Carol had hung up.

The next morning she'd managed to get a number of details about the travel plans from a conversation with Sam. He'd been very open about it, suspecting nothing and telling her everything she wanted to know. As for the people involved, he'd said he knew virtually nothing.

She'd called Kilder back with that information and he told her he had reached his contact in Africa. "His name is Tom Sorrens. He's a very nice guy, a local, and you're in luck. He's got a few thoughts on who these people might be. In fact, he's had an interest in this kind of thing, so he's agreed to look into it. Okay?"

"Fine," Carol responded, "but can it be kept secret?"

"Sure," Kilder said. "But after you arrive, you'll need to slip away from the group and meet with Tom for a few minutes. A little planning session. Then, provided nothing happens, no one will ever know we were there."

Carol had agreed and gotten final instructions.

She'd then hung up and almost immediately Jennifer had called.

Later she'd spent a nearly sleepless night wondering if she had done the right thing.

FORTY-ONE

Shortly after the group had arrived at the home in Africa, when she'd gotten Jesse comfortable and everyone was busy unpacking, Carol had stepped out front and, as planned, she saw a tall, thin black man near a group of small houses and barns across the dirt road. He was standing, smoking, in the shade of a spindly acacia tree beside what appeared to be a barn and small stable. He smiled at Carol, then with a slight gesture of his head, signaled for her to come his way. As she walked in his direction, he threw his cigarette into the dirt and stepped into the barn.

Carol strolled across the narrow dirt road as if getting familiar with the area. When she approached the barn, the door was ajar.

"Carol Drey?" a voice said quietly.

"Yes," Carol replied.

"I am Thomas Sorrens," he said with a heavy colonial accent. "Please just glance around a bit more as if you are perhaps admiring our beautiful area, then step into the barn."

Carol did as he instructed.

Sorrens was an extremely thin man, well over six feet tall, and as black as any African Carol had ever seen. He wore blue work pants and a thin, white polyester dress shirt. He extended his hand. "Hello," he said with a broad smile, "I understand you have a bit of a situation."

He then listened to Carol's story patiently. As she talked, he lit another cigarette, and when she finished, he asked her a series of questions, mostly about who exactly was in the house and specifics about what the plan was. Finally, he stepped to a nearby canvas satchel and removed what Carol realized was a kind of wide elastic waistband, some wiring and a few small pieces of electronic gear. As he untangled the wires he said, "There are a good number of what I suppose you might call 'religious followings' in my country. Most are well-meaning and quite harmless, but there are a few we are very concerned about."

"Why?"

"Because they use drugs to take advantage of people."

"Dale said you had some ideas about who they might be?"

"Yes," he said, moving toward Carol with a clump of black wiring in hand. "I hope you won't mind me wiring you up with my little gizmo."

"A microphone?" Carol asked, suddenly wishing she'd never made the call to Kilder.

"Right. These days it's all getting surprisingly compact. We will need to place this under your blouse."

He waited for Carol to step forward.

She stood frozen. "God!" she said. "Do we have to do this?"

"I am afraid so," Sorrens said with a kind but firm smile.

Again, Carol hesitated.

"You trust these people you are with, correct?"

"Yes."

"Some other people are the bad guys, right?"

"Right."

"And I understand you are doing this because you want to protect your friends and this defenseless boy?"

"Yes."

"Well, this is the best way to do that. We have to be able to listen in. As I said, ma'am, I doubt we will have any problems, but better safe than sorry, right?"

Carol stepped forward.

After strapping the equipment around her waist and giving her a simple set of instructions, Sorrens taped a microphone under her blouse. "Remove it at night," he said, "and put it on first thing in the morning. You turn it off and on right here. That's all there is to it. Oh, and don't wear it in the shower!" he quipped with a smile.

Walking back to the house, Carol felt sick with betrayal.

FORTY-TWO

The van was empty except for several large, colored pillows, two blankets, and a few reed mats rolled up and laid on the seats. As Ona drove, Sam and Christopher did everything they could to calm Jesse, but during the chaos, just as they'd left, he'd become even more panicky. Both men held the convulsing boy between them and secured his legs.

"It's okay, Jesse," Christopher said, trying to smile and stroke his brother's cheek. "It's okay, pal! Hey, buddy, relax!"

Sam also tried to comfort his son, holding him tightly, saying, "Jesse! Jesse, we love you, son. It's all going to be just fine. You'll see!"

For a long time, Jesse would have no part of the reassurances. He continued to wail and shudder for what seemed like an eternity to Christopher and Sam, and soon after they'd gotten on the road, he urinated in his pants. Then, slowly, his panic began to subside. But he was not himself.

He had exhausted himself thrashing about and now began to simply whimper and flinch periodically, staring straight ahead, squeezed tightly between his father and brother.

During this time, Ona kept looking in the rearview mirror as she drove, heartbreak in her eyes. Eventually, even Jesse's whimpering began to subside and he fell into a kind of comatose silence, staring straight ahead, not reacting to Christopher or Sam's attempts to reassure him.

Sam had wanted desperately to talk to Christopher, to tell his son that he was unsure about what they were doing, but it took all of his effort to put on an air of calm for Jesse.

Then the drinks were handed to Christopher in plastic cups. He gave one to Sam and held Jesse's. Son and father stared into each other's eyes and both felt tears welling up. Christopher offered the drink to Jesse, and to his amazement the boy gulped it down as if it were some kind of medicine that he felt would save him from the torment he had been experiencing. Following this, Sam and Christopher both drank immediately.

The van continued on.

The last thing Sam remembered was Jesse whimpering, leaning his head against his father's chest in exhaustion. Jesse was looking up into Christopher's eyes. His brother was smiling down on him, and that was bringing back the good feelings he wanted so desperately to return.

FORTY-THREE

They awoke in the same clearing, surrounded by thick jungle. All three were naked. Jesse lay close to his father and brother—pale, thin, curled in a fetal position. As he began to stir, Sam looked around and saw that Christopher was getting to his feet behind them. To the side, both Sam and Christopher saw the leafy, tunnel-like opening.

Jesse began to roll over, stretching out his skeletal, white limbs. Sam and Christopher knelt beside him. Neither man was sure what the boy's reaction would be. When he had fallen asleep he'd seemed exhausted and paralyzed with fear. The commotion had been nearly unbearable for him, but here there was no noise, no chaos—just the bright, incredible beauty of the jungle.

Jesse looked around, saw Sam and Christopher, and then his surroundings. At first the look of panic and confusion resurfaced. But as he glanced around, his expression transformed into one of first wonderment and then complete amazement. Finally, he looked up at his father and brother arching his neck, rolling from side to side wearing a broad, excited smile.

When Sam and Christopher saw his acceptance, they helped him to his feet and each took one of his arms. As they helped him walk between them toward the opening, he marveled at the clear, brilliant air and the smell and feel of the long grass under his feet. The world became dark and moist under the archway of thick vegetation. The cool stone path led downward. They descended slowly, and all the while, Jesse looked from side to side and up into his leafy surroundings with amazement. Eventually they arrived at the open meadow and the distant, unmistakable sound of rushing water.

"There!" Christopher said.

The three moved, arm in arm, to their right past a group of tall ferns and large, leafy branches. Beyond the layers of leaves, vines, and tree trunks, the bridge stood cloaked in its moist wall of vegetation. As they approached, the sounds of the rushing water swept up from far below them.

Sam took the lead. Christopher came behind him, holding Jesse tightly. The men slowed, and very carefully stepped up onto the bridge.

As they traversed the mossy trunk, Sam suddenly noticed something out of the corner of his eye. He looked down and saw a brightly colored cluster of red and yellow beads that appeared to have been caught on a branch. He thought back to the old woman's satchel. He started to say something, but in the urgency of the moment he simply pointed and then moved past. From behind him he heard Christopher say, "Cheliese..."

A few minutes later all three stepped down onto the damp, grassy earth on the other side.

Sam's heart raced with an exhilarating mixture of anxiety and excitement. Christopher sensed his father's uncertainty. "Dad," he said, "this is it. This is Jesse's time."

Jesse sensed the concern in both his father and brother. But this was overshadowed by his perception of the incredible place surrounding him. Perhaps in his mind he knew something more was about to unfold for him. Whatever his comprehension, he now seemed comfortable and happy to Sam and Christopher, even in his pale nakedness.

The men set out with Jesse between them.

It took very little time before the strange feelings began—the lightheadedness, the momentary flashbacks, the sense that instants had become eons, and, finally, the mental clarity.

During this time, the transformations rose up in their bodies and minds. For Jesse, the human thread existed in a subtle and distant way. His humanity had not been one of intelligence and language for many years. The change he experienced was not only a transformation, but also an incredible release. He could feel himself being lifted out of the restrictive human form he had occupied nearly his entire life, and placed into the body of a physical being that was perfectly suited to this breathtaking place.

As the changes increased in him, his rigid limbs became loose and flexible and he felt his arms and legs filling with a strength and power he had never imagined. He began to move with a smooth, rhythmic motion, and soon felt the release of his father's and brother's hands. The fluidity, the freedom, and the incredible rhythm of what he was now doing became an experience beyond his wildest imagination. And along with the changes in his body, came the changes in his mind. The disabled mind that had never found a way to communicate, to understand the world around him, now began to understand what he was experiencing very clearly, but in a new and exciting way—a way without words or human intellect.

An amazing, exhilarating cadence had begun to flow around and through him, perfectly timed to the subtle motions of a green, fresh, untouched world that had existed in the beginning of man's journey.

Seeing other animals, Jesse saw himself. And in his own very primitive way he realized he had been fully released to become a being who was nearly one of them. He understood their sounds and movements with no need for logic or language. He sensed their desires with no need for reason. He felt their hunger, experienced their fears, and languished in their inherent connection to a source of all universal existence.

As the three arrived at the edge of a clearing, Sam and Christopher stayed back. Jesse moved forward, as graceful and comfortable as any natural being in this wild paradise. The rhythmic beauty of his movements blended in as a complimentary facet of the movements of trees and grass. The gleam in his small brown eyes caught the sun, and the spark soared with the flights of birds and tiny insects. His heavy breath took in the wind and gave it back to the leaves and sky.

And it was in this moment that Sam knew deep in his

heart and mind, he *had* done the right thing. His son had come home.

The boy moved gracefully into the center of the clearing and stopped. A wind swept through his hair and over his dark skin. It carried the smells and sounds of a place teeming with the world's most basic natural rhythms. His wide nostrils filled with the scents of a billion life forms. His dark, wrinkled face reflected the sky and the curtains of life draped before him in the wildness of all creation.

From the edge of the clearing, Sam and Christopher sensed what was happening. Deep inside their now primitive minds, the thread that connected them to humanity told them that Jesse would know the answers. They watched as he squatted in the meadow of long grass, gazing upward into the canopy. As the light slowly began to fade, he laid on his side. Sam and Christopher moved up beside him and also laid down, and as the stars climbed over their ancient world, the three slept.

Just as his father had, Jesse began to dream of the flow of light and images. But for him they were different. He saw the details with brilliant clarity. For him, the curtain of obscurity did not exist. For the disabled son, who years earlier had left behind his ability to speak and reason, the pieces immediately began to fit.

The images of light were not just lines, shapes, or coherent waves of energy and brilliance, they were the swirling language of a creator. And without words or logic, through motion and the senses alone, they began to reveal a story to the young man whose retreat from the world years earlier had prepared him for this moment.

Though he had no knowledge of the questions his father and brother had struggled with, and no intellect to express any answers, Jesse now began to grasp a very primitive comprehension of the human journey. Like a silent, swirling stream of knowledge, forming images that might have been playing out on some celestial movie screen, it conveyed at once that humanity was not unique—that the process of evolution, the motion of life, was happening continually in a vast universal flow, with not just humans, but a myriad of living things. But the span of those events, Jesse saw, were only brief, brilliant sparks—instantaneous bursts of light like the rapid-fire flashes of some great cosmic camera.

To the beings and the races experiencing them, the flashes were taking millions of years to occur. And for those grand moments, those multimillion year instants in time, an actual glimpse of the progression and the essence of all creation was tangible to those who lived them. Sight, touch, smell, hearing, taste...*awareness*—the ability to actually recognize and ponder the work of an ultimate power. Jesse understood without words or logical thought that this was the magic and the blessing of the human consciousness. Through their ebb and flow the shapes told him that all things lived through cycles in their own kinds of existence, and all passed from one form to another as the eons moved by. Few were the fortunate ones whose tiniest elements came together in one brief instant into a form that would allow them to interact with the source of all life.

As the images circled and streamed around him, Jesse also began to recognize that those countless flashes, those single moments, as amazing as they might be to the ones who experienced them, were not the "center" or "focus" of existence. It was not organic life, not the flesh and bones, not the roots or leaves or wings or scales that mattered. These existed in a momentary state that would always be swept back into the flow. All human beings, all living things, would pass though their cycles. They would live and die—some in joy, others in sadness. Some loved and nurtured, others brutalized and tortured. But whatever their brief existence, Jesse knew that their flesh would quickly blend into countless other parts of the moving body of time—trees, rocks, light, water, star matter, gas, galaxies, nebulae—the countless forms of existence continually churning, being transformed time and again, in the passage of eternity.

It was what was *left* when the flesh had passed—what the body and mind had *conceived*—that mattered.

The souls!

He felt them sweep around and through him carrying the experiences and emotions of lifetimes—countless words and acts, hopes and dreams, loves and desires, a conscious awareness of the magnificent universal motion. Each was drawn out of the flesh at the moment of death, and Jesse began to sense that their purpose held the true meaning of existence.

They were an endless outpouring from all parts of the universe—streams of energy drawn into the essence of an unfathomable power as a kind of spiritual fire, driving the rhythms of the cosmos, which, in turn, created more life. The cycle was self-sustaining, and this all-encompassing force, this boundless power of movement and creation, not a being of any kind, was the entity that man had defined as God.

But this brought a paradox.

If the flow of time and all life was God, and if God was not a conscious being… If the cycle was so vast, mindlessly perpetuating itself and everything in existence with no regard, no compassion or focus on the momentary human experience… If human kind was not the beloved child of God…

Suddenly, a flood of knowledge swept into his mind with brilliant clarity.

The lines. The images. The story. They had been produced by a *conscious* entity.

A *second* force was at work.

That force had been close to humanity for countless eons. Mankind was a *part* of an ultimate power too vast to comprehend. But mankind was the *adopted child* of this second entity—a conscious being that cared, watched, and guided. It had turned the race away from the simplicity of the natural world toward an intellectual evolution. There had been a reason for that departure, but a turning point would soon arrive that threatened that purpose. And the story had begun to reveal a solution, a path. As the images swept away, Jesse sensed that he had taken only the first few steps along that path, and before him was a very long journey.

The dream faded.

He slept at peace.

FORTY-FOUR

When the light returned, Sam and Christopher rolled up from the grass and looked toward the center of the clearing. They saw that Jesse was no longer with them.

For a moment, Sam felt his heart quicken. Somewhere, deep in his mind a voice called out, saying, "Your son! The fragile boy you brought to this place naked and defenseless! What have you done to your lost, frightened boy?"

And somewhere, eons in his past, he remembered two women and a bittersweet sadness welled up in his heart. But the human thread was deep and distant, and more prominent now were other feelings. Not rational thoughts, not logical bits of sentences or intelligent deductions. Instead, these feelings were a sense, a gut-feel that his son had gone from them for only a moment, but he had been accepted in this world of living balance and wonderful motion, this world where he was not defenseless, where he fit perfectly, and was finally allowed to be free.

Jesse had gone, but he was not lost. He was close by. And this place, this Eden, was his amazing, new world.

As she lay down in the lush foliage of a sacred world, Cheliese Olafa felt her time of passing approach once again. But this time, that knowledge flooded into her with a sense of pride and completion she had sought her entire life. The story would be told.

In her last moments, Cheliese gave thanks for the gift of life she had received—the wonderful years that had allowed her to witness and take part in the work of God. Fondly, she remembered each of her children, her husband, her parents, and the barren place of her birth. She recalled vividly all the years of wandering and all that she had seen and experienced—that long time that she now knew had only been a moment in a much longer, sweeter journey on which she was about to embark.

With great joy, she felt her flesh going dormant, returning to the state that would allow it to blend back into the stuff of creation. Deep gratitude filled her heart as she felt her last breaths flowing peacefully from her lungs. And at the final instant, the last moment of her life, as she voluntarily released herself from a time and place called Eden, she was suddenly swept up in a flood of joy that she knew she would now experience for the passing of eternity.

FORTY-FIVE

As the white van disappeared in the distance, tears gave way to an overwhelming silence in which Alice, Jennifer, and Carol continued to hold each other for consolation. And with the exception of Carol, the women had no idea that Tom Sorrens' surveillance had gotten underway.

Two days earlier, after Dale Kilder had hung up the phone from his first conversation with Carol, her words kept nagging at him. Not only were the circumstances odd, Carol had also mentioned two words in one breath that had a very familiar ring—Africa and bridge.

Kilder wasn't sure when, where, or how, but he had heard something about the existence of a purported mysterious bridge in Africa. And for some reason he seemed to recall it involved a drug connection. If his memory served him right, a group of religious fanatics had claimed the bridge was some sort of spiritual crossing. What he could not remember was any arrest or conviction activity surrounding it. After hearing Carol's story, however, he decided that it was worth contacting Tom Sorrens in Nairobi.

When Sorrens heard of the family and mention of the bridge, he was immediately interested. What, he wondered, was a man like Sam Waltrick doing bringing his mentally challenged son to Africa to visit this reputed bridge over a spiritual crossing? Because this question was both fascinating and perplexing, and because Sorrens had spent nearly a year trying to verify the existence of a small group allegedly using Spider Eye hallucinogens to run a "Bridge to Eden" scam, when the van pulled away it was being watched by an agent from a nearby hilltop.

And when that agent gave word that the vehicle was in motion, a helicopter, in which Sorrens was a passenger, lifted off. He and his pilot made visual contact with the van almost immediately as they hovered just above a distant tree line. Staying out of eye and earshot, the helicopter followed the van as it left the village and wound through the countryside. As it moved along, Sorrens and his pilot speculated where it might be headed. Both agreed it would probably be the foothills of a small, local mountain range where the Spider Eye grew in abundance.

When the van turned the opposite way and instead headed toward downtown Nairobi, the agents were puzzled. They climbed to a thousand feet, directly over the vehicle, and followed as the skyline of Nairobi drew closer. Not long after this, the van entered the city limits. It wound through a poverty-stricken residential suburb and then crossed a small bridge over a stagnant wash. It turned into an industrial area and finally a vacant lot beside a crumbling, weed-infested parking structure. There it came to a stop.

On the ground, a government car that had also been following, quickly moved into position. The driver and his partner were directed by Sorrens to enter the parking structure and keep the van in view at all times. The driver followed instructions and both men immediately spotted the white van parked in the adjacent lot. Keeping it in sight, they pulled in among several other cars and waited.

For the next hour nothing happened. Sorrens became anxious. Was there a chance the group had somehow slipped out between the time it had entered the lot and the surveillance car had arrived? Not possible. That had been less than a minute. Or, had a meeting been set up and the other vehicle simply had not arrived yet? Or, had the driver somehow realized he was being followed and simply parked, abandoning their journey?

Later, Sorrens instructed his pilot to land the chopper on the vacant, top level of the parking structure. From there, he headed down to the lot. He personally walked by the vehicle, glanced in through the windshield and saw nothing but a black curtain. He passed by again, this time closer, and finally, when he could see nothing, he and several other agents simply walked up to the van and shined flashlights in through the windshield.

It appeared empty.

Preparing to break into the van, they tried the passenger side door and found it unlocked. Inside they found nothing but blankets, mats, and pillows. After several hours of detective work, no one could figure out how the occupants had vanished. Any exit from the vehicle would have exposed them. The lot sprouted several acres of weeds, bamboo, and other vegetation, but the van had parked in an open, dirt area. The group would have been spotted had they so much as rolled down a window.

The agents checked every inch of the lot, inspecting it for tunnels or some other hidden form of escape, but they found nothing. Eventually, they left the scene and placed a lookout near the van hoping to apprehend the occupants when they returned.

But no one came back.

Two days later, the van was towed to a police impound lot where it remained, and was never claimed.

Three months later it was sold at auction.

FORTY-SIX

Because of the bizarre circumstances under which Sam, Christopher, and Jesse Waltrick had disappeared, a full investigation was launched. No trace of the men was ever found. Nor did the authorities discover the reputed bridge or anyone who knew of its existence.

Because Carol Drey had been wearing a "wire," the conversations recorded just before and after the van had left, convinced authorities that she, Alice, and Jennifer had no criminal or harmful intent. Authorities also assumed that Alice had previously been influenced by some form of hallucinogenic agent, possibly Spider Eye spores, and that the entire group had been taken in by some bizarre con game. No charges were filed and the disappearance of Sam, Christopher, and Jesse went in the books as an unsolved crime.

Alice forgave Carol for her "betrayal," telling her goodfriend that by recording the events she had not only tried to protect them all, but inadvertently saved Alice from suspicion. Though she never spoke of, or acted on it, Carol secretly harbored a grudge against Alice for the rest of her life. She felt that no matter how convincing their spiritual encounter might have seemed, including Jesse in their misguided attempt at religious rebirth had been a great mistake and an irresponsible act.

Alice and Carol often spent time together at night in the Constellation Wing, sitting beside Jesse's bed. They would wonder about him, Sam, and Christopher. Alice would talk of the wonderful experiences they must be having, and Carol would smile and reassure Alice that she also believed this. The two women spent the rest of their lives together—twelve years for Carol and fourteen for Alice—living under a shroud of quiet, uneventful sadness.

When her mother died, Jennifer inherited the entire Waltrick estate. After a period of mourning and unrest, she was able to let go. Her career accelerated. As the years passed, she became more and more like her father, a tough as nails business woman who would let nothing stand in the way of her success. Her love and family life was also a great success. The relationship with Aaron blossomed into a deep and lasting marriage that brought beautiful and healthy twins into the world.

One day, five years after her mother's death, as she drove out of her health club parking lot, she decided on a latte for the trip home. She pulled into a local strip mall, found a parking space and walked into a large bookstore complex. On her way to the coffee counter, she passed by the store's massive bank of magazine racks. She glanced to her right and suddenly stopped short in her tracks, eyes locked on a just published copy of *National Geographic*.

FORTY-SEVEN

Though Mitchell Solomon left Waltrick Media Management the day after signing his termination papers, he stayed in touch with his former associates long enough to hear all the rumors about what had happened to his company's founder: Sam had gone off his rocker, went back to Africa and was living like a caveman in the jungles; he had planned it all to get rid of the disabled son that he felt was weak and a failure in life; his wife had conned him into going because she'd had a spiritual awakening; and the most persistent—his flaky son had conned Sam and Alice into the trips to Africa where the three men of the family had disappeared after a mysterious FBI pursuit. This had conveniently left the mother and daughter filthy rich and free from the domineering males who had ruthlessly controlled their lives.

Whatever had happened to Sam, Solomon decided the CEO's definition of "comfortable" had been more than generous.

In no rush to find a job, he knocked around aimlessly for nearly fourteen months. He cruised, took flying lessons, went on safari, and spent ridiculous amounts of money on Hollywood parties and women he hardly knew. As the months passed, he became increasingly arrogant, then moody and angry, and finally depressed.

Eventually, he decided to look for work, assuming all he needed was to get back into a productive routine. In very little time he landed a job with Miller-Stein, a competitor of Waltrick Media Management. At first that brought a renewed sense of energy and excitement, but after a few months, the elation had worn off and Solomon decided to go into therapy.

With the help of his analyst he soon began to realize two things. First, he was not just depressed. Something more was wrong—something had been jumbled or disorganized inside him. Though he had no idea how, he also began to suspect that this problem had originated with Waltrick Media Management. It was during his time there that he had changed. He'd never been able to quite grasp exactly what it was or why it had occurred, but something had happened, something strange...

As the months went by, this conviction grew and festered and Solomon became increasingly haunted by a sensation very much like that of having a person's name constantly on the tip of the tongue but not quite being able to say it. Instead of a name, however, it was an incident, an event—some very simple, but powerful occurrence that had quietly burrowed its way into his psyche...and begun to rot.

His work and personal life provided distractions for short periods of time. He even made an effort to start up a serious relationship with an attractive real estate agent who worked in the same office building. Things began well enough, but soon the bizarre feelings and anxieties interfered, distracting him, and making him more and more prone to spending days at a time completely alone.

The relationship failed, as did another that same year and Solomon realized that with each passing day he was becoming more and more disconnected from virtually everything in his world—people, money, work, and his hopes for a bright future. His bosses and peers eventually recognized this, and before he'd reached his two-year anniversary, he was let go.

The layoff was devastating. It brought back the same feelings of shame and failure that had accompanied his firing from Waltrick. And as these feelings intensified, Solomon began to recall Sam Waltrick's words just after the two shook hands for the last time, "I have a feeling this law business isn't your calling, Mitch."

During the last six months of this period in his life, Solomon could not get those words out of his mind. And as the syllables scraped and squealed in his brain time and again, like fingernails on a mental chalkboard, his pattern of lethargy, drinking, and weight gain grew from a classic, self-destructive lifestyle into a personal sloth and self-loathing that became physically and mentally debilitating.

Despite, or perhaps because of, his steady deterioration, Solomon dropped out of therapy and spent most of the final two months of this period locked indoors. He saw or talked to no one other than the mail carrier, his landlord, the checkers at the local supermarket, and fast-food delivery people.

The last day of his ordeal came on a Saturday.

At 3:30 p.m., he rolled out of bed and walked to the bathroom and then the kitchen. With a fifth of Cutty Sark whiskey and a razor sharp box cutter in hand, he walked back to his darkened bedroom and sat in a reclining chair wearing nothing but his pajama bottoms. Facing a blank wall, he began to drink the whiskey straight and talk out loud to himself, making a case for suicide.

At 4:40 p.m., the bottle was half empty. At 5:23 p.m., the box cutter and the bottle dropped out of his limp hands, and he fell unconscious.

It was early the next morning that everything changed. It began with an obsessive desire to clean his body.

After a twenty minute, blazing hot shower, with his head pounding and his mind still clouded by the previous day's drinking, he began to dry himself in front of a steamed, wall-length mirror. Though he could not see his reflection clearly, he dropped the towel and stood naked and motionless for several minutes facing the mirror. Then, for no good reason, he began doodling lines and shapes on the fogged glass—ovals and rectangles crisscrossed with lined patterns. At first they seemed like random scribbling, but soon he noticed that the shapes seemed to flow out of his mind and through his finger with a kind of order or cohesion. And there was something familiar about them. Something... Someth—

And suddenly, he saw it!

A computer screen—the screen in his office at Waltrick over three years earlier. "*Of course!*" he whispered, his voice beginning to quaver. "*God, yes!*"

He'd seen these same lines one morning moving across his computer screen at Waltrick! He remembered vividly walking into his office sipping his usual morning coffee, and sitting down. He'd looked up and there they'd been, gliding slowly, assembling themselves on the dark glass. Some kind of weird programming mistake he remembered thinking. At first he remembered feeling mesmerized by the lines and drawn in by their odd but soothing motion, then as a reflex, he'd reached forward and hit the space bar. The images vanished. But there had been something strange about them. The way they'd seemed to flow so gracefully and slide into his mind, easing in, almost with a kind of magical, hypnotic cadence. Something...

And he had suddenly realized that the computer was turned off! He'd thought at the time how bizarre that was, and now he recalled something else. It was just after this incident that everything had changed.

Yes, for God's sake!

At that moment!

As he began to draw what would be the final shape, Solomon's hand swept along the smooth, wet surface and his thought patterns suddenly started to change. As his finger slid and squeaked to a stop a final time on the fogged glass, he was jolted by a realization so simple yet so powerful it was like an out-of-body-experience. An involuntary gasp of the words "*Oh, Jesus!*" escaped his lips as he stiffened and slid to his knees:

"You're a good man, Mitch. I think you'll make your mark, but in some other way..."

Jesus! "*You're a good man...*"

In that moment, everything changed for Mitchell Solomon. He quit drinking that day and went back to school. He quickly earned a credential and began teaching.

He loved it.

At first it was entertainment law at a small, community college, but the profession held bad memories for him. He lost interest and began to seek more meaningful academic subjects. He soon took an interest in cosmology which led to ongoing explorations of theology, astronomy, and eventually the subject he found most fascinating—archaeology.

This motivated him to pursue a series of post-graduate studies, a master's degree, and finally, seventeen years after leaving Waltrick, his doctorate. It also laid the foundation for his subsequent work as a noted author and paved the way to a prestigious position at a highly respected, private college in Washington, D.C.

Much to Solomon's surprise, these accomplishments, along with his field work and television appearances, earned him even more extraordinary recognition—an ongoing series of private meetings with the first lady and the president of the United States, both of whom, he discovered, were passionate aficionados of religious history and archaeology.

The meetings began simply enough with a request by phone, a limo ride, and a rather stiff conversation in the White House library. They quickly evolved, however, into a comfortable, informal series of get-togethers in which the three often shared wine and lively discussions about historical discoveries, pertinent literature, and current developments in the field.

FORTY-EIGHT

On this day, Dr. Solomon looked out from the podium over a theater class of two hundred and fifty students. As he opened his laptop and prepared a multimedia presentation, he began telling the group about a place in Africa—a river, a waterfall, and according to recently discovered scrolls, a valley from which all human life on Earth was said to have sprung.

He brought up a Google map of the Kenya area and pointed out the spot near the city of Nairobi, where the river and waterfall were said to have existed. "Here," he said, "is Mount Kilimanjaro. This is part of Lake Victoria, and," as a much closer image appeared, "here's the spot. There's still a river at this location, but it's nothing like what's been described. Today it's more like an overgrown wash called Kifu Maji or 'dead water' that runs along the outskirts of Nairobi."

He zoomed to a closer view of the area. "At this spot a tremendous waterfall once tumbled over a great cliff into a valley."

As he went to an even closer view, now focusing on the river, he continued. "We believe the scrolls describe a waterfall a thousand feet high, and today at this spot there's barely a drop in the river's elevation. And, of course, any valley that might have existed is long gone.

"There are several theories about what happened to the area. The most prominent and logical, and, in fact, the one supported by archeological and geographical research, is that a valley and waterfall did actually exist. But over time—roughly six million years—erosion, ice ages, changes and movements in the Earth's crust have filled up the basin that is now Nairobi and Kenya, and basically leveled the entire area."

A student raised her hand.

"Yes," Solomon said.

"I'm confused. If the waterfall was wiped out millions of years ago, how could anyone have written scrolls about it?"

"Ah!" Solomon responded. "Someone's awake out there! That's a very good question and there's a very intriguing story behind the answer. What we are now calling the Kenya Scrolls were discovered here, in a reed satchel, less than a year ago." As he said this, Solomon brought up an aerial image. It showed a closer view of the river and the buildings surrounding it. He pointed out the crumbling, overgrown ruins of what was once a square, gray parking structure just south of the river. It was beside a vacant lot thick with vegetation.

"Impossible as it seems, radiocarbon dating couldn't be used on the scrolls because they kept dating out as modern era. All indications are they'd been written in very recent times, but in a primitive, in fact prehistoric, hieroglyphic-type language."

A new slide showing two facing pages of the scrolls appeared. "It's an amazing and very subtle form of communication based not just on the graphic symbols used, but how those symbols change positions with respect to one another. To understand this language, you first have to grasp the idea that there is a kind of movement involved and rhythmic patterns created by that movement help convey the ideas.

"These scrolls seem to describe the waterfall, a natural bridge over a gorge, and a number of prominent geographical features that fit perfectly with what modern science has told us.

"And here's another interesting fact," Solomon continued, as he brought up another image. "In addition to the scrolls, our recent digs across the river, here and here, unearthed two skeletons." The parking structure could be seen as a small square at the lower right side of the slide, the river bisected the lower area of the slide diagonally, and in the upper left area, what appeared to be several miles from the structure, two separate archeological excavations were visible.

"These were fascinating sets of bones found at two different locations—not human, but also not simian. They appeared to be the skeletons of two unique hominids—one male and one female. We know they were both very old and strikingly similar to the early primates, but with a few, subtle differences. And extensive research has placed nothing like this life form on record. These two appeared to be some form of very, *very* early humans, quite possibly the first ones. And here's the kicker. Like the scrolls, their bones could not be radiocarbon dated."

Solomon paused and glanced around the room waiting for some reaction. When there was none, he continued. "It's almost as if these two old, simian-like creatures stepped from our modern day world back in time over six million years...and never returned to the present."

The class remained silent.

The screens went dark.

"Eden? The new cradle of life? Some mysterious paradox of evolution?" Solomon smiled and said, "Your guess is as good as mine."

The lights came up.

"But," he continued, "what some are calling the most stunning thing of all, is what appears to be contained in these scrolls. I'm particularly excited about this because I'm honored to have been chosen to lead a small, highly respected group who will undertake the full translations. We're just now beginning a long and difficult task, but early results appear to be profound. They suggest that the scrolls may present a completely new theory of God, man, and creation."

Again, though Solomon waited for a reaction, there was none. Or, perhaps there had been, he suddenly thought. He could have heard a pin drop in the room.

"You are all well aware of how profoundly the religious conflicts are now affecting our lives," he continued. "Whatever your spiritual beliefs, you've been witness to the last decade—the confluence of religious animosity, nuclear proliferation, and political aggressions that have brought us to a precipice. You know that unless we come to a common understanding about our world, our God, and for God's sake our politics, the terrible conflicts that are taking lives as we speak in all major countries of the world—including our own—will very soon threaten our existence. My colleagues and I are lucky enough to have unique accessibility to key world leaders, and we are in hopes that these scrolls will somehow offer a solution to this dilemma. If they do, we feel confident we can make a convincing case for world consensus...and peace."

And with that, Dr. Solomon excused the class. He then packed his teaching materials and left the room.

Two floors down from his classroom, he stepped out of the elevator and turned the corner starting down the long, gray, linoleum hallway toward his office. He immediately noticed a woman sitting on one of the chairs just outside his office door. He could see that she was an overweight blond in her fifties or sixties. Hearing his footsteps, she looked up. Though she was still a good distance away, under the harsh fluorescent lights Solomon immediately recognized something odd in her stare.

FORTY-NINE

"May I help you?" Solomon asked as he approached the woman.

"Dr. Mitchell Solomon?" she asked, getting to her feet.

"Yes."

She held out a magazine with a wide, yellow border. Solomon looked down and saw the most recent copy of *National Geographic*. On the cover was a close-up shot of one of the pages of the Kenya Scrolls. The lead story tease line read: "The language of a creator? Page 46." Solomon took the copy of the magazine and beamed with pride.

"Yes," he said, "it's just out. They sent me advance copies."

Assuming now that she was simply an admirer and she was probably waiting for an autograph, he continued, "May I help you?"

"Turn to page 46," she said.

Solomon opened the magazine to page 46. For a moment he was confused. It was the title page of his article.

A large color photograph revealed a dig site in Kenya with him standing over it, supervising a group of students. But lying on top of the page, like a torn, crinkled book mark, was a brittle piece of paper. After a moment, Solomon realized what it was—a shred of wallpaper with the pattern side facing down onto the pages of the magazine.

He paused and looked at the woman. She said nothing.

He reached for the piece of paper and turned it over. It was blue with a whimsical cowboy pattern. Obviously for a small child, he thought, probably a young boy. But over the top of the pattern was a cluster of shapes drawn with crayons. For an instant, Solomon didn't absorb the impact of their existence. They were ovals and rounded rectangles, drawn in red, broken lines that looked very similar to—and suddenly, it hit him like a kick in the stomach.

He drew a quick breath, feeling his temples constrict.

He turned up to the woman.

"My name is Jennifer Waltrick-Madison," she said. "That piece of wallpaper was torn off the wall in my brother's bedroom nearly forty years ago."

Solomon looked down. He closed the magazine and held the piece of wallpaper beside the cover photo of the scrolls. There was no doubt. The strokes, the shapes, the accents. They were part of the same language. His heart pounded.

"Please..." he said, barely able to get the word out as he stepped forward, unlocked his office door, and showed the woman inside. "Can you please—" He stopped and turned. "Waltrick?"

"Yes."

"I'm, I... Good God!"

Jennifer sat down and told Solomon the entire story.

When she had finished, he appeared dazed. After a moment, he stammered, trying to gather his thoughts, and finally said, "Your father's medical and dental records. Will you release them for our review?"

Jennifer nodded.

"And if we need your DNA?"

"I'll be happy to give you a sample."

Solomon stared at her. He knew exactly what he must do next. "Jennifer? May I call you by that name?" he asked, getting to his feet.

Jennifer nodded. "Yes, of course."

Solomon led her to the door. "Thank you," he said. "I'll be calling you very soon. At this moment I have important work to do."

FIFTY

Nearly a month after his meeting with Jennifer, Mitchell Solomon stepped out of the elevator into the university administrative building and walked down the long hall toward an executive conference room. The door was open and seven people were seated inside around a large oval table. Four were holy men: a rabbi, a monk, a cleric, and a priest. The remaining three were the dean of the School of Archaeological Studies, a noted linguist, and an award-winning field archeologist.

Solomon entered the room and took a seat.

"Well, Mitchell," the dean said. "I'm glad you're sitting down. We have news."

"Some good, some bad," the cleric added.

"Yes?" Solomon asked, glancing at each of the faces.

The rabbi slid two newspapers across the table. "First the bad news," he said. "In case you haven't already seen them."

One was a *New York Times*. The headline read, "Christian Coalitions Launch Global Crusade!" The second was a *Los Angeles Times*. Its headline read, "Muslim Armies Vow Nuclear Annihilation."

"It looks as if the day we've all been dreading may be close at hand," the dean said.

"And the good news?" Solomon asked.

"Your new friend is on the level. Her DNA is a match. The bones of the old male are her father's, Samuel Waltrick, a businessman who—with his two sons—disappeared in Kenya some twenty years ago."

Solomon was stunned. "And the old female?"

"An African woman named Cheliese Olafa."

"But this is—"

"We know," said the archaeologist. "It's not possible. But neither are fossilized remains that date out as modern era."

"How did you verify the old woman?"

"Sketchy medical records of her as a child in Ethiopia and, as you suggested, we tracked down a hospital stay in Nakuru late in her life. Turns out she was born with a deformed right foot—two fused bones—just as our ancient skeleton has, albeit in the skeleton's case, very close to the opposable thumb of a nearly simian foot."

"That almost cinched it," the priest added, "and led to a DNA comparison with her only surviving child, a daughter. She's a match."

FIFTY-ONE

"Hello?"

"Hello, Jennifer? It's Mitchell Solomon."

Jennifer placed the broom aside and sat down at the breakfast counter in her kitchen. "Yes."

"You said there was another woman. Ona?"

"Yes."

"I'm hoping to find her."

"It's been years. And I never knew her."

"I believe you said she was from the United States."

"Yes. That's what my parents told me. I think she came to Ethiopia with the Peace Corps during several severe drought years. It would have been in the mid-eighties, I think. Have you found something?"

Solomon drew a breath and leveled his voice. "The male bones were your father's. The old woman was an African. Both had undergone profound physical transformations."

Jennifer felt her chest tighten. "My God! It *was* true?"

"Yes. And do you realize what that means?"

"Christopher and Jesse."

"There's a good chance they're still alive." Solomon waited for a response. When he got none, he continued, "And if we can get back there and find out where this place is—how this was possible—I can't begin to tell you how important this could be—especially right now."

Jennifer glanced over at her daughters, both sitting at the kitchen table doing homework.

Six days later, Solomon and Jennifer stepped into a small restaurant called Rofu, in the heart of Nairobi. Solomon approached the hostess and said, "Solomon. We have a reservation."

The woman did not pause or look down at her reservation list. She simply said, "Yes, this way, please," and led the couple toward the back of the restaurant.

Walking under a smoky haze, through dark red lighting, the pair passed rows of black leather booths and worn wooden tables, then rounded a corner. They saw a slight female figure wrapped in colorful cloths, seated in the shadows of a rattan-framed alcove at the rear of the room. The hostess gestured and Solomon and Jennifer stepped forward.

Ona was very thin, with short, now graying hair, high, round cheekbones, and large liquid eyes. Her face had aged and wrinkled, but the elegant beauty of her symmetry and lines had not diminished. She wore traditional African dress with colorful beads and ivory rings. Smiling as the pair approached, she stood and said, "Dr. Solomon?"

"Yes," Solomon answered. "And this is Jennifer Waltrick-Madison."

Ona looked at Jennifer for a moment, and then smiled. "It's a pleasure to finally meet you," she said.

"Thank you," Jennifer replied.

"Please sit," Ona said, then turned to Solomon. "Professor, you've come here with profound and perplexing questions."

"Yes," Solomon said.

She then turned to Jennifer. "Jennifer, I understand you hope to reunite with your brothers after many years."

"Yes."

"I can take you both now to the place you've been seeking, but please understand something. If you come with me today, your lives will be profoundly and *irreversibly* changed."

Jennifer and Solomon looked at each other. Tears came to Jennifer's eyes. She turned back to Ona. "Are they...are both my brothers alive?"

"Yes."

"Are they happy?"

"Very happy. And they both love you very much."

"Can they come here? Just *meet* with me?"

"I'm afraid not."

A few moments later, all three got to their feet. Solomon hugged Jennifer, then pulled back and looked into her eyes. "I'm not sure what happens now. But I do know that none of this has been by chance... Go home now to your family."

Jennifer sat down, her tears spilling over.

Solomon and Ona left the restaurant through a back door.

ACKNOWLEDGMENTS

Though a number of people have helped make this book possible, a few have had a significant impact on its development, and to these people I am especially grateful. One is Phillips Wylly, a fine writer and filmmaker with frank opinions and a keen eye for story line and characterization. My son, Sean, has also offered excellent criticism and much encouragement, as have my wife, Patti, my brother, Guy, and my good friends Andy and Jason Boyer. I am indebted to my colleagues, Ralph Phillips, Ned Rodgers, and Remy MacKenzie. All took the time to read the manuscript in its early stages and offer suggestions that helped me shape a rough, initial draft into the story presented in these pages. Sandi Hathcock, another good friend, also offered early support and criticism. Though less direct, the love and support of Sunday, Shawn, Riley, Sidney and Karic Grennan, have also helped me greatly. Finally, the staff at Cambridge House Press, especially Rachel Trusheim, have done an excellent job with the editorial development, design work and countless other technical and creative elements required to place this book in your hands.